CRISIS

"Meg," her teacher said, and she looked up. There was something strange in his expression as he gestured toward the door, and she gulped without knowing why, a tight coldness starting in her neck and throat.

She stood up, clenching her pen hard enough to hurt her hand, and crossed to the door. Something's happened, I know something's happened. Please don't let anything have happened.

Her agents were standing in the hall, and feeling their concerned urgency, the coldness turned into a hard contraction of fear.

"Who is it?" she asked unsteadily.

"Your mother," one of them said.

WHITE HOUSE AUTUMN

Ellen Emerson White

AN AVON FLARE BOOK

AVON BOOKS
A division of
The Hearst Corporation
105 Madison Avenue
New York, New York 10016

Copyright © 1985 by Ellen Emerson White
Published by arrangement with the author
Library of Congress Catalog Card Number 85-90673
ISBN: 0-380-89780-6

First Avon Flare Printing: October 1985

AVON FLARE TRADEMARK REG. U.S. PAT. OFF. AND IN OTHER COUNTRIES,
MARCA REGISTRADA, HECHO EN CANADA

Printed in Canada

UNV 10 9 8 7 6 5 4

This one, is for my father.

WHITE HOUSE AUTUMN

CHAPTER ONE

Meghan Powers slouched in the back of her Current Issues class, incredibly bored. Her friend Alison yawned at her from across the aisle and Meg nodded, feigning death from boredom. Top *that*, Camille.

"Miss Powers?" her teacher asked. "Do you have a problem?"

Meg sat up hastily, death scene arrested. "Sir?"

"I realize," he spoke with some sarcasm, "that a discussion of the Presidency can hardly be expected to hold your interest—"

Most of the class laughed.

"*But*," he continued, "I would appreciate it if you would try to pay attention."

Meg blushed. "Yes, sir," she said. She was going to add, "Forgive me, sir," but he might not find that as amusing as she would. When you were the President's daughter, you kind of had to watch your public behavior. Her mother had only been in office for nine months and Meg was still trying to get used to it. They all were.

She slumped down into her turtleneck. Turtlenecks were good to hide in. But this was a nice skiing shirt and she probably shouldn't stretch it out. She sat up, turning to check the clock. Ten minutes to go. Major drag. It was only October and she wasn't supposed to have senioritis yet. However.

Maybe she would look at Josh for a while. She liked to look at Josh. Except that he was looking at her and it was too embarrassing to stare back. Besides, staring lovingly was sort of a public display of affection and one wanted to maintain decorum whenever possible. That made up for the times when it *wasn't* possible. Like during the last song

1

at dances. Amorous embraces seemed rather appropriate at such moments. Except for White House dances. Although officials who had had a little too much to drink had been known to break that rule. Like Raul, the prince who had taken their association as dinner partners as an engagement or something, and spent the whole night trying to kiss her until Preston, her father's press secretary, had tactfully tangoed her away. Meg liked Preston.

The bell was ringing and she closed her notebook. That was the good thing about thinking—you could kill a lot of time. Not that she ever accomplished much. *Reflections*, by Meghan Powers. Swell. She and Rod McKuen could walk off into the sunset together. *Admiring* the sunset.

"You coming?" Josh asked.

"Yeah." She zipped her books into her knapsack and smiled back at him. He had a very nice smile. And nice hair and nice eyes and a nice nose—the kind of person you would ask for directions; although, knowing Josh, he would get rattled, blink a lot, and send you blocks out of your way. Not miles, just blocks.

"What are you thinking about?" he asked.

She grinned sheepishly. "I don't know. Things."

"Interesting things?"

"Yeah." She walked closer to him in the hall, smelling his after-shave. It was pretty funny to imagine him putting on after-shave in the morning when she knew he didn't shave. Or, as he put it, he shaved every three months, whether he needed to or not.

"I'm sorry I can't come to the match."

"It's no big deal." She automatically swung her arm as if she were holding her tennis racket. "I don't think we'll beat them anyway."

"Nice attitude, captain."

"Well," she glanced around, "don't quote me."

He made his hand into a microphone. "Yes, fans, you heard it here. Miss Powers admits—"

"Funny," she said, pushing him off-balance. Actually, it was too true to be funny. Reporters were always showing up at her matches and *People* had even printed a hideous picture of her hitting a dropshot. On the run, mouth open, eyebrows furrowed. Really most attractive. And embarrassing. It was like, she spent thirty hours a day trying to get everyone to forget who she was, and one stupid picture would blow it in about thirty seconds.

"You can beat Melissa Kramer, can't you?" he asked.

Melissa was the other team's number one player. "I don't know." Meg sighed. "I mean, she's ranked and everything."

"You gonna smash them, or what, Meg?" their friend Nathan shouted down the hall. Nathan was six-four and one of the few football players she had ever genuinely liked. He had huge shoulders and arms, a close-cut Afro, and always wore those baseball shirts with brightly colored sleeves.

"Six-love, six-love," she shouted back.

"Boy, some people sure are conceited," Josh said.

Meg laughed, pushing him again. "You're really a jerkhead, you know that?"

"You tell me all the time," he said, nodding.

"Mrs. Ferris says for us to get ready as fast as we can," Alison said, meeting them at Meg's locker.

Meg missed the last number of her combination and started over. "Big pep talk?"

"And how," Alison agreed. She looked at Meg, at Josh, then grinned. "I'll see you in the locker room."

Meg flushed. "Uh, yeah. I'll be right there." When she had her books and was waiting for Josh, she wandered down to the corner where Wayne, one of her Secret Service agents, was. "I'm just going to change, and then head out to the bus."

He nodded. On days when she had away tennis matches, two extra agents would come so that her regular two could ride on the bus with her and the others could follow behind in a car. At the beginning of the season, the Secret Service had wanted her to ride in a separate car, away from the rest of the team, but Meg had protested so vehemently that, luckily, the Secret Service had compromised. Having her agents on the bus was bad enough, especially when everyone was talking about sex. Which was most of the time. No wonder they lost so many matches.

Josh walked her to the locker room and they paused outside, near the drinking fountain.

"I'll call you tonight," he said.

She nodded. "Have a good lesson." Two afternoons a week, he worked with his piano teacher, preparing for auditions for the conservatories he was applying to, even though he insisted that he would never get in and would end up majoring in economics somewhere.

"Have a good match." He leaned over to kiss her and Meg made sure that no one was around before relaxing against him. Well, her agents were around, but they never looked. "Do it for the Gipper," he said against her mouth.

"I'll do my best, Knute." She hugged him, then pulled away. "Talk to you tonight?"

He nodded, kissed her once more, and she went into the locker room.

They lost the match and someone from *The Washington Post* took pictures of her perspiring and lunging for cross-court shots. Her opponent had good placement and Meg had a hard time beating her, the match going to three sets before she finally pulled it out with some of her very hardest serves.

She was ranked first on the team, which made her uncomfortable, as if it were only because she was the President's daughter. In fact, when she'd first tried out for the team, even though she knew she could beat the current number one player, Martha, she carefully lost her challenge match so she would be ranked second and not have to feel as if she had been given special privileges. But her coach had not been fooled and kept her after practice to accuse her of throwing the match. Meg had allowed as how maybe she could have done better and Mrs. Ferris had said that if she were going to throw matches, she wouldn't be able to be on the team at all. Awkwardly, Meg explained the situation and her coach sympathized, but said that she couldn't be on the team with that attitude.

Meg decided to adjust her attitude, but she still threw points sometimes because most of her opponents were uneasy about playing the President's daughter and Meg didn't want any unfair advantages. Nothing like winning a few points to make people stop feeling uneasy.

Her agents left her in the North Entrance Hall, with its shiny checkerboard floor, marble pillars, and flashy main staircase. Meg usually went up the main stairs instead of the private staircase because the main one ended up near the Center Sitting Hall where her bedroom was. There was an elevator, but she never took it. When in doubt, burn up calories.

She dumped her racket and books on the bed, messing up the quilt and pillows a little. She made her bed before she went to school in the morning—her parents insisted—but the maids always remade it, much more neatly. Neat beds made Meg nervous.

"Hi," she said to her cat Vanessa, who was asleep among the pillows. Vanessa purred, extending a soft gray and white paw, and Meg smiled. "Pretty cute," she said and batted her hand against the paw a few times. Vanessa liked games.

"Are Neal and Steven around?" she asked, changing out of her red and white tennis shirt and into a very old green chamois shirt that had once belonged to her father. Her shower could wait—first, she had to have a Tab. "Here, come on." She picked Vanessa up, balancing her in the crook of one arm. "Let's go see what's going on."

"Miss Powers?" A butler, George, came down the hall to meet her. "May I bring you something? A Tab?"

Meg grinned. Nothing like having everyone know how your mind worked. "Sounds great," she said, following him down to the kitchen so she could at least take the glass out of the cupboard and feel as if she were helping. The White House staff didn't like you to help them, but Meg felt like a jerk being waited on all the time. Armed with a delicate crystal glass of Tab, she went up to the third floor solarium where her brothers were slouched in front of the

5

television, watching "The Brady Bunch" and eating chocolate cake.

"Hi." Steven gave her his usual arrogant eighth grade grin, his feet resting on a maple coffee table. "You sure look ugly."

"Yeah, and everyone thinks we look *just* like each other." Meg sat down on the other couch, next to Neal, who was eight and hadn't learned about arrogance yet.

"I think she looks pretty," Neal said, smiling up at her, and Steven pretended to throw up on a cushion before focusing back on the television.

"Oh, yeah." Steven picked his head up. "Jerky Beth called before."

"Beth's not a jerk," Meg said automatically. Beth was her best friend from home and they had a tendency to call each other a lot. "Did she leave a message?"

"Something about the essay questions for Wesleyan, I don't know." He picked up his cake. "Hey, d'ja win or lose?"

"Got her in three sets." Meg swung her legs onto the coffee table. If there was anything she enjoyed wearing, it was sweat pants. She infinitely preferred herself in sweat pants and old flannel or chamois shirts. "Which one is this?" She indicated the television.

"When they go to the Grand Canyon," Steven said with his mouth full.

Meg nodded, looking at him, then at Neal. It was funny the way the three of them did and didn't look like each other. She and Steven were like their mother, with very dark thick hair and narrow, high-cheekboned faces. Neal was more cherubic, with light brown hair and a gentle smile like their father's. Even so, you could tell they were related. They all slouched the same way. It had to be more than that, but the slouching was obvious. Her parents were always bugging them to shape up on their postures.

"I like the one where they go to Hawaii better," Steven said, getting up and disappearing into the little room just off the solarium to wash frosting smudges off his hand. He had this habit of not using plates or forks when he ate cake.

A rather disgusting habit, in Meg's opinion, but then again, she only ate the creamy part of Oreos, so she figured she wasn't one to criticize.

"What's for dinner?" he asked, coming back out, using Neal's head for a towel.

"Roast beef," Meg said. "And I think, Yorkshire pudding."

"Blech," Neal said.

"It's not that bad." Meg broke off and ate a small piece of his cake. "And it's Mom's favorite."

"Is she coming to dinner?" he asked.

"Far as I know." Meg offered Vanessa some cake. Vanessa wasn't interested, so she gave it to Kirby, their dog, who was on the couch with Steven.

"What about Daddy?"

Steven grinned. "He had to go shake hands with Miss Cherry Blossom."

Neal giggled and Meg had to grin, even though she felt sorry for her father because of all the annoying things he had to do. Like cut ribbons in front of new buildings, plant trees with Cub Scouts, address the Senate spouses. In real life—well, life before the White House—he had been a tax attorney.

They sat through "Happy Days" and were watching "M*A*S*H" when their father came in, dignified in a grey worsted suit, with a muted red tie for contrast.

"How was Miss Cherry Blossom?" Meg asked.

His smile was wry only if you knew him. "Very excited."

"Did you kiss her?" Steven asked.

"We shook hands." Their father took off his jacket and Steven put it on, sitting up and trying to look like an adult. Their father loosened his tie, then sat down, pulling Neal onto his lap and frowning at the television. "Filling your little minds with garbage again?"

Meg looked at the ceiling. "Forgive him. He knows not what he says."

Her father smiled. "You all could be in your rooms,

reading Dickens." He tilted his head at Neal. "How was school?"

"Fun," Neal said.

"What did you do?"

"Kickball."

"All day long?"

Neal giggled, then nodded.

"Terrific," their father said. "The school's not even giving you Dickens." He looked at Meg. "How about you?"

"I don't know." She slumped down in her best teenage punk imitation. "Got drunk again."

"Terrific." He tipped her Tab glass to study what was left of the liquid and Meg jerked the glass away, guzzling it and falling back in a drunken stupor. He laughed, then leaned over to look at Steven. "How about you?" he asked. "What did you do all day?"

"Read Dickens," Steven said solemnly, getting a giggle from Neal, a smile from their father, and a groan from Meg. He glanced away from the television just long enough to cross his eyes at her.

"Ah," their mother said from the doorway. "There you all are." She came in, tall and, as always, beautiful, in a blue silk dress, slimly belted in at the waist, and wearing graceful high heels. No wonder her father hadn't kissed Miss Cherry Blossom.

"Guess what, Mommy?" Neal asked. "We played kickball! All day!"

"Well, that sounds productive," she said, smiling.

Watching her cross the room, Meg meditated vaguely on the fact that she would probably never meet another woman with her mother's skill on high heels as long as she lived. Meg generally fell off espadrilles, forget high heels. She also fell off things like sneakers and Topsiders, and if it happened in public, would pretend that she suffered from a severe inner ear problem.

"Hey, Prez," Steven said.

"Hi," Meg said, sitting up straighter and no longer pretending to be drunk.

"Hi." Their mother smiled at them, bending over to accept the hug Neal offered. She looked at their father over Neal's head. "Good evening, Russell," she said in her most dignified voice.

"Good evening, Katharine," he nodded, equally dignified, and they exchanged one of their long private looks that always made Meg feel as if she shouldn't be in the room.

"Madame President," George said from the door, "may I bring you anything before dinner?"

Her mother decided on white wine, her father concurring, and George left, returning a few minutes later with the wine and a platter of cheese and crackers.

"I must say," their mother let out a sigh that meant she was going to relax for a while, "I've been looking forward to this all afternoon."

"Rough day?" their father asked, covering her hand with his.

"No rougher than usual, I suppose." She closed her eyes for a brief, apparently rejuvenating, second. She opened them, looking at Meg and her brothers. "So. Tell me what you all did in school today."

"Dickens," Meg said.

CHAPTER TWO

Meg sat in bed that night, patting Vanessa and reading an Allen Drury political novel. She was supposed to be working on her college essays, but after an hour on the phone with Beth—who kept saying things like, "How about we blow off this whole college thing and just go out to Colorado or someplace and be disreputable for a few years?"—she wasn't in the mood anymore. Besides, questions like, "What message, in twenty-five words or less, would you send to the inhabitants of another planet?" were kind of holding her back. What did they want her to write? "Hello from Earth. Having a wonderful time. Wish you were here." Of such answers, college acceptances were not made. Not that the President's daughter wasn't going to be accepted. Terrific. Nice to be accepted or rejected on her own merits, or lack thereof.

Someone knocked on the door and she considered hiding her book and running to her desk to bend industriously over essays, but figured she wouldn't be able to pull it off.

"May I come in?" her mother asked.

"Yeah. Sure."

Her mother opened the door, closing it behind her. The President in her lounging gown. Yes, Virginia, Presidents *do* wear bathrobes.

"What are you reading?" she asked.

Meg held up her book and her mother nodded. Meg read a lot of political fiction and nonfiction. Like, almost exclusively.

"The man has a very depressing view of it all," she said.

"The man is not completely off-base," her mother said.

Meg arched one eyebrow, putting on a "pray, continue" expression.

"Oh," her mother waved that aside, "I'm just tired. Long day, that's all."

"Would you like to talk about it?" Meg turned her right hand over to use it as a make-believe note pad.

Her mother grinned. "No, thank you, Doctor."

"Do you feel alone? Friendless? Persecuted?" Meg kept the note pad ready.

"You read a few too many books, my dear," her mother said.

"Yeah, I finished a really swell one yesterday." Meg reached onto her night table for *Witness to Power*. "It's about this President named Nixon, see, and—"

Her mother just rolled her eyes.

"It was really good."

"I can imagine." Her mother sat at the bottom of the bed. Very nice posture. "How's everything going?"

"Fine, thank you," Meg said politely. "And you?"

Her mother leaned over to cuff her. "Seriously, Meg." She recrossed her legs. "How are things going?"

"Josh asked me to the Homecoming Dance."

"Big surprise," her mother said.

"I said yes."

"Even bigger surprise," her mother said.

"It's semiformal."

"What are you going to wear?"

"Can I borrow your Inaugural gown?"

"Don't you think it might be just a trifle sophisticated?"

"Maybe a trifle," Meg said, sitting up and trying to look as mature as she could in her Talking Heads T-shirt.

"I think so," her mother agreed. "I'm sure we can come up with something more appropriate."

"I prefer black evening wear."

"We'll see."

"I'm not leaving the house in pastels."

"Oh, but I had my heart set on rose," her mother said.

"I'm not leaving the house in pastels."

Her mother laughed.

"Well, I'm not."

"Fine," her mother said. "We'll just have the dance here."

Meg sighed deeply, although the thought of her high school coming to the East Room in frumpy dresses and leisure suits was an amusing one.

"Well, okay," her mother said. "If not pastels, I'll settle for mauve."

Meg sighed so deeply that Vanessa woke up. "Sorry," she said, patting her.

"In all seriousness." Her mother leaned back against the bedpost, folding her arms, and Meg visualized the caption that would go with that pose: The President caught in a rare moment of relaxation. "I thought we might discuss your interview."

Meg shuddered. *Seventeen* was coming to interview her the next day and she could think of about nine thousand ways she'd rather spend the afternoon. Like raking leaves or cleaning the cat box or having her appendix out or—

"Preston will be sitting in with you, of course," her mother said, "but I thought you might want to talk about it."

"I thought I might just kill myself," Meg said.

"You'll be fine. Just remember to count to three before answering questions."

Meg grinned. "What if I forget and count to four?"

Her mother also smiled. "You'll look rather daft. Three is just long enough to plan your answer."

"May I quote you?"

"What, and give away my trade secrets?" Her mother reached over to give her another cuff which Meg reacted to as theatrically as possible, lying dazed and unconscious against her headboard. Her mother kept talking, giving no indication that she had noticed. "You might want to watch your grammar," she said. "If the woman has a poor ear for dialogue, you might come across as a bit of a ruffian."

Meg frowned. "You mean, I can't say 'ain't'?"

"I mean things like 'going to' and 'have to' as opposed to 'gonna' and 'gotta.' "

"I don't say 'gotta,' " Meg said, offended.

"If you were speaking quickly, you might. Just be careful."

Meg nodded, the thought of the interview making her feel very sulky. Not like a good little trouper at all.

"As I said," her mother continued, "I'm sure you'll be fine, and Preston will be there if you need help."

"I guess," Meg said, feeling fretful enough to give her mattress a little kick. "I probably can't make jokes or anything either, right?"

"You might want to watch it," her mother agreed. "It's altogether possible that she won't appreciate your sense of humor."

Meg grinned sheepishly. Sometimes she had the feeling that there were a lot of people like that.

"Not that *I* don't appreciate your sense of humor," her mother said.

Meg made her grin shy.

"To a degree."

Meg made her grin sad.

"A small degree." She glanced at Meg's empty desk. "How are your essays coming along?"

Meg patted Vanessa.

"Have you started them?"

"Um, well." Meg frowned. "The one to the Barbizon School is almost finished."

Her mother humored her by nodding.

"Would you like to read the one I'm doing for Juilliard?"

Her mother sighed. "You don't play an instrument."

"Oh, but I sing. Haven't you heard me sing?" Meg grinned. "Want me to do 'I Got Rhythm'?"

"No, thank you."

" 'I got rhythm, I got music, I got—' "

"It *is* October," her mother pointed out. "Those applications are going to be due before you know it. Especially," she glanced at her hands, "if you apply anywhere early decision."

Radcliffe. Her mother's alma mater. And her father had gone to Harvard for law school. Not that they were pushing her or anything. "I don't know, Mom," she said. "I don't think I want to apply anywhere early decision. I'd rather try for a lot of different schools."

"Then you really *do* have to start working," her mother said. "That's a lot of essays."

"You want to see the one I wrote for Oral Roberts?"

Her mother laughed. "No, thank you."

"Well, how about the one for—"

"Have I ever told you that you are perhaps the most annoying person I know?" her mother asked pleasantly.

"Not that I recall."

"Mmmm." Her mother smiled. "Well then, perhaps I should—"

There was a knock on the door.

"Yes?" her mother asked.

"There's a call for you, Madame President," Felix, another butler, said. "Secretary Brandon."

"Thank you, I'll be right there." She kissed the top of Meg's head. "Excuse me."

"Tell him I think we need to take a more aggressive stance in Cuba," Meg said, imitating her mother's presidential frown of concern.

Her mother smiled again. "I'll give him the message."

As usual, the conversation at lunch the next day centered around where people were applying to college, who was going to get in where, what schools were good, what schools were hack. Meg kept her mouth shut during conversations like that. Sometimes she felt as if she spent a good portion of her *life* keeping her mouth shut.

She looked around the table, sipping her milk. Except for Alison, most of her friends were male, which was strange because at home in Massachusetts, it had been the opposite. She had always been kind of nervous around the opposite sex. Shrinking Violet. *Stuttering* Violet even. But here, a lot of girls seemed to see her as a competitor, especially insofar as boys were concerned. Meg had figured that that would die down after a few months, but even now, she would see girls take their boyfriends' arms when she walked by. Kind of a pain. Competition like that gave her an ulcer.

She spent most of her time hanging around with Josh, Alison, Nathan, and another friend of theirs, Zachary, who was a basketball jock and a trombone player. Even *better* than the Gang of Four.

"So, you getting the cover or what?" Nathan asked.

Meg stopped sipping milk, seeing that he was looking at her. "Who, me?"

"Seventeen."

"God, I hope not." She glanced at Alison. "You doing anything this afternoon?"

"Going to the dentist."

"Want to pretend to be me and *I'll* go to the dentist?"

"Meg Powers, Young Woman in a Hurry," Zachary said solemnly and they all laughed, Meg imagining a picture of herself in a floppy hat and raincoat, fleeing madly.

"Here," Josh said, handing her an Oreo. "Maybe if you eat this, you'll have cavities by two-thirty."

"No such luck," she said.

The bell rang, and as they were walking up to the dumpster to throw away their trash, he put his hand on her arm. "Are you really that nervous?" he asked.

"Yeah, kind of."

"You've done interviews before."

"Not anything this big a deal." Her parents almost always turned down interviews because they thought "focused publicity" was asking for trouble. Preston sent out occasional news releases—"Today Meghan took her SATs" or "Steven was three for four in his baseball game," but her parents wanted the three of them to have as little exposure as possible, for both security and privacy. Meg wasn't supposed to know about the percentage of letters, out of the stacks she got every week and usually spent Sunday afternoons trying to answer, that were obscene and/or threatening. The staff screened her mail first, but she had overheard people talking about some of the sick letters she had gotten. No one ever mentioned it directly.

Except once. In July, some horrible revolutionary group had decided that they wanted to kidnap her and had mailed all kinds of threatening letters and made phone calls and everything. She had been confined to the White House for over a week, everyone treating her like a little bundle of dynamite. She wasn't supposed to go out on the Truman Balcony, she wasn't supposed to walk around on the lawn, she wasn't supposed to do anything. What she did, was pace nervously around the house. Her parents had been extremely upset and, to counteract that, Meg tried to be cheerful and make jokes and pretend that none of it was happening. Since they had yelled at her for taking it too lightly, she was pretty sure the bravado had worked. She had tried to handle the whole thing with a certain panache. Humphrey Bogart all the way. Luckily no one knew that she had gotten sick to her stomach almost every time she ate. Even now—like right now—when she thought about it, her stomach hurt.

But nothing had happened, and gradually, her security eased back to its normal level. She really only thought about it when she was in the car with her agents and they were at a red light. If a van pulled up, she would get scared to death, gripping the door handle, expecting terrorist commandos to come leaping out with machine guns and drag her inside. Drag her inside and—God, she didn't even want to think about it.

Anyway, her parents had agreed to the *Seventeen* interview because it seemed pretty safe, and if she did one big interview, they could refuse all of the others. Major ones, anyway. Little things would be printed—like photos of Neal out at recess or Steven and her father shooting baskets. Steven had also gotten his picture in *Tiger Beat* as a "new teen heartthrob" and been impossible to live with for a couple of weeks. Once, a picture of her leaving a movie with Josh had shown up in *Life*. The President's daughter with regular escort Joshua Feldman. One pretty funny picture had been when she and her family were up at Camp David and some photographers took pictures of the three of them swimming for part of a story about her mother which included "The President's children at play." Meg had been wearing a somewhat skimpy two-piece bathing suit at the time and had had to stay under water so the photographers wouldn't get her from the neck down. The photographers had thought she was a bad sport.

"What are you thinking about?" Josh asked, holding the cafeteria door for her.

"The stupid pictures I'm going to have to pose for."

"What are you wearing?"

"I'm supposed to 'dress conservatively.' "

"Says who?"

"The parents."

"They're right." He rested his hand on her waist. "The country would get too excited otherwise."

"Right."

"Would I lie to you?"

"I don't know."

He smiled at her, the sweater she had given him for his birthday, a sort of coppery russet, bringing out the color of his eyes. "What do you think?"

"I think you're cute," she said.

CHAPTER THREE

Conservative clothing. She decided on a blue plaid wool skirt, a white Oxford shirt, navy blue knee socks, and her Topsiders. She was going to wear a headband, but it made her look about eleven. She would have to stick to wavy and wild.

The phone next to her bed rang and she picked it up.

"I have a message from Mr. Fielding, Miss Powers," the chief usher said. Mr. Fielding was Preston.

"Is *Seventeen* here?"

"Correct," the chief usher said. He was the man who pretty much ran the White House. "Shall I tell them you're on your way?"

"Yeah," Meg said. "I mean, please. I'm just going to brush my teeth and everything."

For one last touch, she yanked a navy blue crewneck out of her bottom dresser drawer to drape around her shoulders for the "casually conservative" look. It took her three tries to make it look casual. Sporty even.

"You want to come?" she asked Vanessa, who was purring sleepily to herself. Except that was pretty contrived. If she was going to go for the cat cuddled to her cheek, she might as well wear the headband. "Maybe you'd better wait here," she said. "Sorry."

Preston and the reporter were in the solarium with a bearded photographer. The reporter was a woman in a brown herringbone tweed suit and oversized aviator glasses. Gloria Steinem greets the Eighties. Preston had on black slacks, a light gray shirt with a skinny black silk tie, and a darker gray jacket over it, his handkerchief perfectly folded in the outside pocket. Very stylish man. He saw her and stood up.

"Meg, this is Kelly Wright," he indicated the woman, who was also standing now, "and this is Ed Crouthers," he indicated the photographer, who nodded shaggily at her.

"How do you do, Ms. Wright," Meg said. "Mr. Crouthers."

"Please," the reporter said, her smile friendly. "Just call me Kelly."

"Oh. Okay. I'm Meg." They probably already knew that.

"I had them bring a Tab for you," Preston said, gesturing towards the tea tray.

"Thank you." Meg picked up the glass, noticing that everyone else had coffee. She was going to have to learn to like coffee. Holding it made her feel older.

Preston sat in an easy chair perpendicular to the couch and Meg hesitantly took the place he had vacated, very self-conscious, trying not to flinch as the camera flash went off. She would not do well at the Barbizon School.

"You have a beautiful view," Ms. Wright said.

"Yeah," Meg agreed, automatically looking out the windows at the South Lawn and the Washington Monument beyond. "I mean, yes, we do."

"I gather that you all spend a lot of time in this room?"

"Yeah—I mean, yes," Meg said. Her mother was right about the ruffian. "Pretty much. I mean, what with the VCR and all." She coughed nervously, glancing at Preston, who gestured with one hand for her to relax.

"What I thought we'd do," Ms. Wright drank some coffee, "is sit here and talk for a while and I'll just ask informal questions. Does that sound all right to you?"

Meg nodded, hands tight in her lap. She hated interviews. Publicity definitely wasn't all that it was cracked up to be. At least Preston was here—he spent most of his time running interference for her father. There had been a big media splash when her father chose Preston, the very suave, very cool black guy to be his press secretary. Preston was always making fun of her father—whom he called "Russell-baby" in private—for being bourgeois, and for

Christmas had given him a subscription to *Gentlemen's Quarterly*. It always amused Meg to see her father on a Saturday morning, slouching in old corduroys and a flannel shirt, reading *GQ*. Steven took a picture of him once.

"How do you feel about living in the White House?" Ms. Wright asked.

"Um, well." Meg tried to think of something profound, or at least interesting, to say. "I don't know. It's, uh, it's pretty big." Great. That put her in the finals of the Inane Remarks of the Year contest. If only she had some anecdotes. They probably wanted anecdotes.

Kirby came nosing out from underneath the coffee table and without thinking, Meg handed him a butter cookie from the tea tray.

"You have five animals?" Ms. Wright asked.

Meg nodded. "I think the cats are downstairs." Kirby wagged his tail and she gave him another cookie. He was one of the first White House dogs ever who didn't live in a kennel outside; luckily, her mother had put her foot down on that particular White House tradition. When they had gotten Kirby seven years earlier—at the pound; her parents believed in that—they had been assured that he was a German shepherd, but he had grown up into a large brown shaggy dog with odd splotches of white. Her mother said he was a collie; her father thought he was mostly retriever; Steven insisted that he was part Airedale. Meg usually just said that he was brown and white.

"Let's see." Ms. Wright checked her notes. "You have two Siamese, a tiger cat, and the gray one is yours, right?"

Meg nodded. "I found her at the Chestnut Hill Mall when I was thirteen."

Ms. Wright smiled. "What was she doing at the Chestnut Hill Mall?"

"She was in Bloomingdale's," Meg said, forgetting to count to three. She blushed. "I mean, I guess someone abandoned her and the ASPCA said it was okay for me to keep her."

Mr. Crouthers decided that he would like a picture of

Meg with her cat, so Meg went downstairs to get her, returning and posing for a few pictures. Cute and contrived. Ms. Wright began asking more directed questions then—about friends, hobbies, White House routines.

Meg answered them, saying that she liked skiing, tennis and reading. Reading what? Oh, anything—political novels, classics, whatever was around. No romances? No, Meg said. What would Josh Feldman say about that? He'd laugh, Meg said, and then went on to answer questions about Josh; about how he was in her class and he was a really good pianist and baseball player and yeah, it was kind of serious, but not really serious. She glanced at Preston to see if she should maybe elaborate on that, but he shook his head.

The questions got harder. Like, how did it feel to be the only daughter of the first female President of the United States. Unique, Meg was going to say, but she counted to three and said "challenging," instead.

"In what way?" Ms. Wright asked.

"Um, well." Meg thought. "I guess everyone has to work harder. To be a family, I mean. To make time for everyone else."

"Would you say that you have a good family?"

"Well, yeah." Meg shifted uneasily. "I mean, *I* think so."

"How do you and your parents get along?"

"Fine," Meg said. Classic cautious answer.

"You never argue?"

"Well, sometimes," Meg conceded. "It's nothing major though."

"What sort of things do you argue about?"

Foreign policy. "Well," Meg glanced at Preston, who nodded. She drank some Tab, planning an answer. "I don't know. About bedtime." She looked at Ms. Wright, who nodded for her to continue. "I mean, I usually stay up pretty late and sometimes my parents grump and say I'll never be able to get up in the morning."

"Are they right?"

"Sometimes." Lots of times. *Most* of the time. Her

mother, who always woke up instantly, couldn't understand why other people might have trouble.

"What else do you argue about?" Ms. Wright asked.

Damn it, she's not going to let me off this one, is she? "I don't know." Meg broke a butter cookie in half, in quarters. "If my room's a mess. If I'm screwing around"—she flushed—"I mean, fooling around instead of doing homework." She looked at Preston, who motioned for her to relax, that they knew what she meant.

"What about drinking and marijuana?" Ms. Wright asked.

Meg counted to six. "What about them?" Steven had once told a really obnoxious reporter that he was a methadone addict and it had taken some quick work on Preston's part to keep it from being printed.

"A lot of young people today—"

"I don't," Meg said. That would be all she needed—to show up in *People* or somewhere, drunk at a party.

"Because of your position?"

Come on, enough already. "Because I don't want to," Meg said, barely keeping the irritation out of her voice. "The people I hang around with aren't into that."

"What *are* they into?" Ms. Wright asked pleasantly.

Whips and chains. "You know," Meg shrugged. "Movies, parties. The same as anyone else."

"What about your boyfriend?"

"Well," Meg shifted, "we go to movies mostly."

"I mean, do you and your parents discuss your relationship?"

"Well, yeah. Sure."

"Are your parents as liberal in practice as they are on paper?"

Count to three. Count to five even. Like Mom says, you'll do okay in an interview if you control the pace. "Of course they are," Meg said. "They wouldn't be very honest otherwise."

"What about premarital sex?"

She's getting mean. "In what sense?" Meg asked.

"What do you think about it?"

Meg coughed so she wouldn't say that she thought about it constantly. "I think it's a subjective issue."

"How do you feel about it personally?"

"It would depend on the situation."

"How so?"

"Come on," Preston stepped in. "Are your readers really interested in that sort of thing?"

"How many teenage girls do you know?" Ms. Wright asked, her slight smile indicating that she knew she had overstepped her bounds. "What about college, Meg?"

One, two, three. "I'll probably be applying to six or seven schools and then, it'll depend on where I get in."

"Oh, come on." Ms. Wright lowered her glasses. "You're not expecting to have any trouble, are you?"

"College admissions are a pretty subjective thing," Meg said.

"Like sex?" Ms. Wright asked and Meg laughed.

The interview got a little better after that, and Meg answered questions about her parents, her brothers, her Secret Service agents.

Ms. Wright scanned her notes. "Just one more thing. Do you have any advice you'd like to give other girls your age?"

"Advice?" Meg stared at her. "Like what?"

"You tell me."

"What, you mean like, something inspirational?" Meg laughed. "You're kidding, right?" She saw that Ms. Wright wasn't laughing. "You're not kidding?" What was she supposed to talk about—good citizenship? She could spout about economic recovery, but Preston would get mad.

"You can't think of anything?" Ms. Wright asked.

"Well—no." Meg played with her Tab glass. "If I start talking about—I don't know—social responsibility, I'm going to sound like a real jerk."

"Do you think there's a need for social responsibility?"

Meg hesitated. "Is this on the record?"

Ms. Wright laughed, shutting her notebook, capping her felt-tip pen. "No," she said. "It's not on the record."

Meg smiled uncertainly.

They ended up going downstairs, running into Steven and one of his friends, who were eating ice cream and laughing raucously, Neal tagging after them. The photographer took some pictures, Ms. Wright asked some questions; then, finally, they left. After accompanying them to the East Wing Lobby, Meg sank into a lattice-back love seat, exhausted.

"Well." Preston sat down next to her. "That wasn't so bad, was it, kid?"

Meg just groaned.

CHAPTER FOUR

"Preston tells me you were quite the political kid today," her father remarked at dinner.

"Yeah," Meg said. "Neal, can you pass the salt, please?"

"How did it go?" her mother asked.

"Okay. Kind of embarrassing."

"Did they ask any terrible questions?"

"Yeah."

"Boy," Steven reached across the table to take the salt as Meg finished with it, "you should have seen Meggie when they started taking pictures. Throwing her hair and everything." He imitated her. "She loved it."

Meg blushed. "I did not. I hate having my picture taken."

"So how come you were throwing your hair?"

"I wasn't."

"Yeah, sure." Steven stuffed half a roll into his mouth. "When that photographer guy asked you to, you did."

"Well, he asked me to."

"What *else* did the photographer ask you to do?" her mother wanted to know.

"Nothing."

"D'ja tell them about the centerfold yet?" Steven asked with his mouth full.

"Steven, cut it out." She tried to kick him under the table.

"I saw her," Neal giggled. "She was throwing her hair."

"Neal, shut up." She tried to kick him instead, but he moved his legs out of the way.

"It wouldn't hurt to have a sense of humor, Meg," her father said mildly.

"It wouldn't hurt to have them shut up either," Meg said, scowling at her brothers.

"Steven, have you decided whether or not you're going to try out for basketball?" their mother asked. Ever the diplomat.

"Dunno," he shrugged. "Coach says I'm too short."

"Yeah, really," Meg agreed. "Talk about munchkins."

"Meg, shut up!" Steven tried to kick *her*. "It's not my fault!"

"Meg, act your age," their father said.

"Oh, yeah," she nodded, picking up her fork. "He harasses me for ten hours, and I get in trouble for saying one thing. Yeah, that's fair."

"Come on," her mother said. "Let's not fight at the table."

Meg put her fork down. "Can I ask you something? Why's it matter if we fight at the table? I mean, what's the difference if we fight *away* from the table, or at it?"

"Yeah, really." Steven also stopped eating. "What's the difference if we're going to fight anyway?"

"The difference," their father said, very patient, "is that your mother and I like to relax at dinner, not listen to a lot of wrangling."

"But we like to wrangle," Neal said.

Their mother sighed, passing her hand across her forehead.

"Want some of my Valium?" Meg asked.

"No," her mother said. "I do not want some of your Valium."

"I've got Librium too. You want some Librium?"

"What's Librium?" Neal asked.

"Remember those blue pills I was giving you the other day?" Meg asked. "Those were—"

"Wait," Steven interrupted. "You were giving him red pills. I don't remember any blue pills."

"Really? Hmmm." Meg frowned. "Maybe they were

26

amphetamines then. Are you sure, Steven? I really thought I was giving him Librium."

"No," Steven shook his head. "You were giving *me* Librium."

"Kate, why don't we go have some coffee?" their father suggested, looking across the table at their mother, who responded with a tired nod.

"You'll be missing out," Steven said. "We're going to take this act on the road."

Their father stood up. "The sooner, the better."

"Yeah, see if *you* get tickets," Steven grumbled.

When their parents were gone, he stopped slouching, sitting up with his elbows on the table. "What's with them?" he asked. "They're pretty grumpy tonight."

"We were pretty bratty," Meg said.

"I thought we were being funny," he said. "Funnier than usual even."

Neal looked worried. "Are Mom and Dad mad?"

"No." Meg finished her squash. "I think Mom's just tired and Dad thinks we gave her a headache. You know how he is."

"But, is he mad?"

"I said no already." Meg held out her plate. "You want my beets, Steven?"

He made a gagging sound.

Meg held the plate under the table. "Want my beets, Kirby?"

Kirby sniffed the cold purple vegetable, then went back to sleep.

"Would any of you like dessert?" Felix asked, coming in to clear the table.

"I'm all set, thanks," Meg said, carrying her plate to the kitchen, Steven and Neal following suit.

"Do we have any cookies or anything?" Steven asked.

Felix smiled a nice grandfatherly smile. "I'm sure we can find something."

After hanging out in the kitchen for a while to eat cookies, Meg left to see what her parents were doing. She found her father by the fireplace in the Yellow Oval Room, drinking coffee.

She sat down in a yellow and white antique chair. Louis XIV. Or maybe it was Louis XVI. She wasn't into furniture. "Where's Mom?"

"Down in the Treaty Room," he answered. "She's trying to get some work done, so don't bother her."

"I wasn't going to," Meg said defensively. "Why are you in such a bad mood?"

"I'm not."

"Oh. Well," she stood up, "sorry I came in here."

"I didn't say for you to leave."

"You don't look too thrilled about me staying either."

He sighed, then smiled, patting the sofa cushion next to him. Meg hesitated, then sat down.

"I'm sorry," he said. "Your mother and I are just tired."

"I'm sorry we were being jerks at dinner."

"You weren't being any jerkier than usual." He let out his breath. "Your mother has a very high-pressure job."

"I know. So do you."

"I wouldn't say that there's a comparison." He leaned back into the cushions, eyes on the ceiling.

"Do you hate it here?" she asked.

He turned his head just enough to look at her. " 'Hate' is a rather strong word."

"Do you intensely dislike it here?"

He laughed, reaching over to ruffle her hair. "I'm fine. What about you? Preston said that they gave you a pretty rough time."

"Kind of."

"He also said that you handled it like a pro."

"Not really."

"He certainly thought so."

Meg shrugged, looking at the fire.

"I worry about you," her father said.

"About *me?*"

"You're very hard to shelter."

"Dad, I'm seventeen. I don't need sheltering."

"I just don't want to see you change," he said quietly.

She tilted her head, confused. "What, you mean, grow up?"

"I don't want to see you turn into a politician."

"You married one."

He nodded, looking in the direction of the Treaty Room.

"Are you guys having a fight?" Meg asked uneasily. She hated it when her parents fought. They never did it in front of anyone, but there would be taut antagonism in the air, buried anger that made her feel as if she were in an invisible maze where she couldn't bump into any of the walls or open any of the doors.

"No, I just—" He shook his head.

"Just what?"

"I don't know." He picked up his coffee cup, sipping some. "They don't have any bright ideas about putting you on the cover, do they?"

"I don't think so."

He nodded. "Good. Your mother and I wouldn't permit that."

Meg grinned. "Because I'm too ugly?"

"Well, that too," he said, putting an affectionate arm around her shoulders.

That meant that he thought it would be asking for trouble to have her on the cover. Scary thought. She folded her arms across her stomach, concentrating on not remembering the week she had been confined to the White House.

She looked in the direction of the Treaty Room, where her mother was busy being the President. She would be sitting at the end of the black walnut table, right hand clenched around a silver pen, telephone balanced on her shoulder, papers everywhere. Maybe switching from her contact lenses to her glasses while she waited for the aspirin to work on her headache. The headache Meg and Steven and Neal had given her.

"Thinking great thoughts?" her father asked, smiling.

"Not really." She looked up at him. "Does she like being the President?"

"Most of the time."

"Yeah." She thought about that. "Do you wish she wasn't?"

"That would be like wishing she were a different person," he said.

Meg grinned with the right side of her mouth. "Should I take that as a no?"

"Very definitely." Now *he* looked in the direction of the Treaty Room. "Hard to share her with the rest of the country, isn't it?"

Meg nodded.

"I think it's worth it though, don't you?"

"I guess," Meg said, less certain. It was worth it to the country—at least, in her opinion; but her family sort of lost out. It would be a lot easier if her mother were a teacher, or a lawyer or something, and they could live quietly in Massachusetts.

"Think of your friends, Meg. Every family has situations to which they have to adjust."

Meg considered that. Josh's parents were divorced. So were Beth's. That was the major family problem people seemed to have, but certainly, there were lots of other kinds of problems. Maybe it was just that living in the White House was so—unique. There were groups for people involved in divorce or alcoholism or—she could see it now: First Families Anonymous.

"It's not *that* bad, is it?" her father asked.

"No. Just different."

He grinned. "It *is* that." He reached over to move her hair back. "Is Josh coming over tonight?"

"To study," she said.

"To watch 'Hill Street Blues,' you mean."

"Oh," Meg tried to look vague, "is that on tonight?"

"Very convincing," he said, then studied her. "How are things going with him?"

"Good. I mean—" She searched for a better way to phrase it. "I guess he's my best friend."

He nodded. "That's the way it should be."

"Is it with you and Mom?"

"Absolutely," he said.

CHAPTER FIVE

Josh came over a little before nine and they went to the West Sitting Hall. Her parents weren't too thrilled about the idea of him being in her bedroom. The West Sitting Hall had a huge double-arched window that looked out over the West Wing, the Oval Office, and the Executive Office Building. Kind of a nice view. It was also one of the only rooms in the house with furniture from their house in Massachusetts—the coffee table from their sitting room, the couch and love seat from their living room, various lamps. It was probably Meg's favorite place in the White House, except for the solarium maybe.

"The interview was okay?" he asked.

"Lots of fun," she said, starting to move her hair back off her shoulders. She thought about Steven making fun of her for throwing her hair around and lowered her hand.

"When's it going to be in?"

"I'm not sure. December or January." Unconsciously, she lifted her right hand to move her hair, saw what she was doing, and frowned at it.

"What's wrong?"

"Nothing." She put her hand down, blushing.

"What are you so embarrassed about?" He moved the hair for her. "I think it's cute when you play with your hair."

"I don't play with my hair."

He grinned.

"Well, it gets in my eyes."

"I think it's cute." His hand moved from her shoulder to her face. "It's also sexy," he said more quietly.

"It is, hunh?"

"Yeah, it is," he said, sitting much closer.

"Hmmm." She brought her hair forward, then threw it back with a sweeping gesture. "How sexy?"

"*Very* sexy."

"Oh, really?" She threw it back again.

"Stop it," he said. "You're making me crazy."

She threw her hair back a third time.

"Okay." He put his glasses on the table. "You asked for it."

"For what?"

He pushed her onto her back, kissing her, both of them laughing.

"I may ask for it more often," she said.

"Well, let me tell you," he kissed her, "I'll—"

"Christ," Steven said, coming in from the Center Hall. "Is making out all you guys ever do?"

They sat up quickly, Meg straightening her hair, Josh putting on his glasses.

"You're lucky I'm not Dad," Steven said.

"Yeah, well, what do you want?" Meg asked, trying to recover her dignity.

"I just came downstairs. Can't a guy come downstairs?" He grinned and sat on the couch between them. "So, how's it going, Josh?"

"Fine," Josh said.

"You've got yourself a good little woman here." Steven put his arm around Meg. "You know that, don't you?"

"Steven, will you get out of here?" She moved away from his arm.

"I just want to know his intentions. Can't I ask his intentions?"

"You can get out of here, that's what you can do."

"Well, okay." Steven stood up. "I'll leave you two kids alone." He grabbed Josh's hand, shaking it firmly. "Come down to the office sometime, boy. We'll talk."

"Thank you, sir," Josh said. "I'll do that."

"Good." Steven nodded several times, starting for his room. "We'll talk."

"The kid's a maniac," Josh said, watching him go, walking like an elderly Supreme Court Justice.

"The kid's a *pain,*" Meg said.

Josh nodded and she knew he was refraining from saying that he thought the two of them had the exact same sense of humor. They wandered up to the solarium to watch "Hill Street," alone. Steven and Neal had either gone to bed or were watching television downstairs. "Hill Street Blues" was Meg's favorite show and she always watched very seriously, not talking, not looking away from the action. Josh humored her, only finding it necessary to kiss her during commercials. When the eleven o'clock news came on, the top story was about the President and her policy reaction to the recent drop in interest rates.

"Do you want to watch this?" he asked.

"I don't know. We could just go down and *ask* her, I guess." She took off his glasses, putting them on herself. "What do *you* want to do?"

He leaned forward, pushing the glasses on top of her head.

"We could listen to a record," she said just as he was about to kiss her.

He stopped, his arms resting on her shoulders. "Do you *want* to listen to a record?"

"Do you?"

"If you want to. Do you want to?"

"If you do."

He kissed her and slowly they moved until they were lying on the couch.

"I could just walk right out there and get one," she said. "Some nice Iggy Pop or some Twisted Sister or—"

He kissed her harder.

"Or," she said when she got her mouth free, "I could just stay right here."

"You could do that," he nodded.

"Unless you want to hear some Lawrence Welk. You want to hear some Lawrence Welk?"

34

He moved to kiss her neck and she decided that it would be much more pleasant to stay right where she was.

"I'm going to take off my sweater," he whispered. "Okay?"

She nodded, not even wanting to let go of him for that long, and he sat up, pulling the crewneck over his head, then moving back down on top of her.

Wow. She slid her hands over his shoulders and down his back, feeling the muscles and the warmth of his skin through the Oxford cloth. Wow. Why did she always get excited so quickly? Maybe there was something wrong with her.

His breathing was faster and Meg could feel and hear herself breathing almost as quickly. She blushed, embarrassed by the sound, a blush that made her face feel even hotter. His hand was inside her shirt and she wondered if it was supposed to feel that good, or if there really was something wrong with her. Well, Meg, she could hear their family doctor, Dr. Brooks, saying, I'm sorry, but it looks like a case of terminal libido. How long do I have, doctor? she would ask, choking back tears. Three months, he would say. Make them good ones.

Hearing Josh's heart pounding, she hugged him closer, ruffling one hand through his hair, affection and passion mixing somewhere inside her.

"I wish—" He sighed, resting his head against hers.

"What?"

"I don't know." He rolled onto his back, bringing her with him. "I wish we could go somewhere where I didn't have to be scared that the President of the United States was going to walk in."

Meg laughed. "I'd be *more* afraid of the First Gentleman."

"You know what I mean."

Now, she sighed. "Yeah, I guess."

"You know what I mean," he said.

"Yeah." She turned her head enough to look at him. "If we went anywhere else, my agents would have to be there."

"Yeah, I know." He sighed again.

"It's not my fault," she said defensively.

"I know it isn't." He rested his hand on her face, running his fingers along her cheekbone. "I'm sorry."

"Don't *apologize*," she said, starting to feel a little testy.

"I'm sorry, I won't." He stopped. "I mean—"

She shook her head, amused. "I know what you mean." She ran her hand across his chest, very much liking the fact that he had hair on it. Like the Marlboro men. She loved the Marlboro men. "If you want," she said, "I could tell you some jokes."

He relaxed too. "You don't know any jokes."

"I know lots of jokes."

He grinned. "You always say that, but you never tell me any."

"I'm afraid of offending you," she said. "Most of them are anti-male, anti-Jewish, anti-musician, and anti-people with glasses."

He nodded. "That kind of cuts me out."

"I don't tell them so I won't hurt your feelings."

"Right," he said and kissed her.

"If you want," she moved to a more comfortable position so her arm wouldn't fall asleep, "instead of listening to records, I could sing for you."

"You're getting in a weird mood," he said.

"Yeah."

He sat up, reaching for his glasses.

"I have these spells," she said. "It's because I was born in Salem."

"You were born in Boston."

"At the State House," she nodded. "My mother was giving a speech."

"And you finished it because she was tired."

She turned to look at him. "I've told you this before?"

"Lucky guess," he said.

They both laughed and he leaned over to kiss her.

"I should probably go," he said. "It's pretty late."

"Yeah. Thank you for helping me with my physics."

He grinned. "Don't mention it."

After walking him downstairs and saying a very chaste good-bye because of the doorman, Meg went back up to the second floor, heading for the kitchen to get some Oreos, and maybe some cheese for Vanessa. When she came out, her mother was by the door to the Presidential Suite, holding a cup of coffee.

"Did Josh leave?" she asked.

"Yeah, just a minute ago."

"I would have come out to say good-night, but," her mother gestured towards her bathrobe.

Meg nodded.

Her mother glanced at her watch. "Does his mother mind him getting home this late on a school night?"

"I don't think so."

"Was there something interesting on after 'Hill Street Blues'?"

"The news," Meg said.

Her mother looked at her watch again.

"We were listening to records," Meg said, embarrassed to feel herself blushing.

Her mother nodded.

"Um," Meg changed the subject. "You want to watch David Letterman? It's Viewer Mail tonight."

"It's a little late," her mother said. "Don't you think you'll have some trouble getting up tomorrow?"

So far, this conversation wasn't going very well. "Yeah, probably." She edged towards the Center Hall. "I guess I'll go to bed."

Her mother nodded. "Sleep well."

"Yeah, you too."

"Meg?"

She turned.

"You *are* as mature as I think you are, aren't you?"

Meg resisted the urge to ask how mature her mother thought she was. "I'm not sure what you mean," she said, taking an Oreo apart to eat the middle.

"Meg, I'm not trying to invade your privacy. I just—" Her mother frowned. "Worry."

"Well," Meg said, for lack of anything better to say.

"Is that it?"

"Well, kind of. I mean, we—well, it's—" Meg sighed. "Want an Oreo?"

CHAPTER SIX

Even in the White House, life could be routine. Meg spent the next couple of weeks concentrating on the tennis team and having long discussions with her parents—which, on her part, mostly involved listening—about where she should apply to college. Right now, she had it narrowed down to Harvard, Yale, Brown, Williams, Stanford and Georgetown, although Beth had been lobbying pretty heavily for Wesleyan, Sarah Lawrence and Hampshire. Meg's parents were still pretty heavily in favor of Harvard.

Right after school started, she and her father had visited a bunch of schools, mostly Ivy League—a trip the media adored. Like at Yale, Senator Quigley's son had taken her on the tour. *Newsweek* and everyone loved human interest things like that. Meg was sort of inclined towards Williams: off in the mountains, away from publicity, near skiing. Harvard would be pretty much exactly the opposite.

Around the house, things were pretty quiet. Her mother was tense and distracted, worrying about the recent flare-up in the Middle East, and the summit meeting at Camp David after Thanksgiving. People like chancellors and prime ministers were coming and it was really a big deal. Her mother had gone to Berlin and London and Paris in May, but this was the first time that major foreign officials were coming to the United States during her administration.

Her father was doing environmental stuff—working to save endangered species, conserve natural resources, fight acid rain. Her mother had a great Secretary of the Interior, and he and her father spent a lot of time together. Meg had this theory that her father's secret ambition was to be a forest ranger.

Steven had made the basketball team, although he probably wouldn't get to play much. He spent every waking moment dribbling. The only place he was allowed to do it in the house was the North Entrance Hall. The doormen and guards really got a charge out of it and kept giving him tips.

Neal was mad because the Secret Service didn't want him trick-or-treating. He could go if the agents came up to the door with him, but he wouldn't be allowed to eat any of the candy. Steven thought this was uproariously funny until it occurred to him that this year he wasn't going to be able to go out and throw eggs or whatever delinquent thing he and friends in Massachusetts had done.

Her mother's solution to all of this was to have a Halloween party—a costume party—to which Steven's and Neal's friends would come. Meg thought *this* was hysterically funny until her father came up with the bright idea that Meg and some of *her* friends could dress up and be chaperones. The press thought it sounded wonderful and the networks and several magazines were planning to come and cover the event. Meg was kind of hoping to contract the flu. Alison had suggested that they all come as characters from *The Rocky Horror Picture Show*, but Meg was thinking more along the lines of showing up as the Pope. She hadn't told her parents yet.

The week before the party, the day the tennis team was playing the one school with the first singles player she knew she couldn't beat, she had a little trouble getting up, a problem which she suspected was Freudian.

The switchboard had to call three times before she said, "Okay, I'm up," and meant it. She crawled out from underneath her quilt, stared out the window and was instantly depressed. The sky was gray, with rain threatening. When she had watched the news the night before, the weatherperson had *insisted* that it was going to rain from midnight on, which would mean that the tennis match was canceled. From the looks of the sky, the storm wouldn't start until right after she lost.

Very grumpy, she opened her closet to decide what to wear. There weren't any rules, but the President's daughter was supposed to try to look nice if she could, not that Meg ever tried very hard. Today, she felt like looking mean as hell, but that was probably out of the question.

She stared at the dresses, skirts, nice corduroy pants, nicer flannel and wool pants, respectable jeans and disreputable jeans. She stared at all of them, then took a pair of navy blue sweat pants out of her bottom drawer. She put them on with a light blue LaCoste and a darker blue chamois shirt as a jacket. Not in the mood for socks, she stepped into her Topsiders. All of this made her feel somewhat less grumpy and she went over to her bookcases to find something she could read a few chapters of, and be completely cheered up.

She pulled out *Coming Attractions*, which was an hysterically funny book by Fannie Flagg, and fell onto her bed to read before breakfast.

"Hey, Meg!" Steven bellowed down the hall. "Dad says you'd better get down here!"

She looked at the clock, scowled, and slammed the book down.

"Meg, come on!"

"I'm coming already!" Twice as grumpy as before, she slouched down the hall to the Presidential Dining Room. "Morning," she grumbled, reaching for the orange juice.

"Snap it up," her father said. "You're going to be late."

Meg scowled and poured her juice so quickly that she spilled some on the tablecloth and had to blot it up with her linen napkin.

"Boy, talk about stupid," Steven said.

Meg kept blotting so she wouldn't throw the glassful at him.

"What are you wearing?" her mother asked, and Meg could hear bad mood in her voice too.

"Sweat pants." She took the Frosted Flakes box from Neal, who was reading the back of it.

"Well, go change," her mother said. "I don't want you going to school like that."

"Like what?" Meg filled her cereal bowl and started reading the box herself, which made Neal kick her under the table. "I always dress like this."

"Not in public you don't."

Meg read the box.

"Dad, make her give it back!" Neal said. "I had it first!"

"Give him the box, Meg." Her father sounded very irritated. "And go put on something presentable."

Meg let out a hard breath, returning the box as ungraciously as possible.

"Ground her," Steven advised, his mouth full of English muffin.

"Shut up," Meg said, "or I'll tell them you're the one who broke the eagle vase."

Her parents scowled at Steven who mouthed the word "bitch" across the table at her.

Their mother put down *The Post* that her aides had highlighted. "It was that basketball, wasn't it? From now on, you're not to use it anywhere in the house, got it?"

"Not even in the North Entrance Hall?" Steven asked. "You promised I could—"

"Well, I changed my mind," their mother said, picking up her paper, her mouth tight.

"That's not fair! You promised!"

"Look, Steven," their father said. "One more word and you're going to be the one who gets grounded."

Steven sat glowering for a silent minute, then looked across the table at Meg. "Bitch," he said, grabbed the basketball on the carpet next to his chair and ran out of the room.

"Steven!" Their father jumped up. "Get back here!" He spun to face Meg. "See what you started? I hope you're happy."

"I didn't start anything," Meg said. "He's the one who—"

"You started it," Neal said.

"I did not! You just—"

Her mother's paper slammed down. "Meg, I don't know what your problem is, but I'm in no mood for it."

Knowing that she was going to get herself grounded for about thirty years if she stayed in the room, Meg pushed away from the table.

"You're not to leave the house until you change," her father said.

She kept going and he grabbed her arm.

"Starting right now, you're grounded," he said. "For two weeks, and if you don't shape up by then—"

"Big deal." Meg shook her arm free. "What's it matter if I can't leave the house without stupid agents anyway?"

"You want me to make it a month?"

"Do what you want," Meg said and left the room. She got her tennis racket and knapsack from her bedroom, meeting her mother on her way out.

"I said for you to change." Her mother's voice was calm, but angry.

"I don't have time—I'm late."

"I'll write you a note."

Meg looked at her, tall and determined, in a gray flannel Brooks Brothers dress with white pinstripes, and sighed, going back into her room. She put on a different pair of blue sweat pants and came out.

"Satisfied?" she asked and her mother looked so furious that she backed up a step.

"Meg, I'd advise you to get back in there," her mother said, her voice so quiet that Meg couldn't help being a little scared. "Now."

Meg swallowed, afraid to push it any further, and yet not wanting to back down either.

"*Now,*" her mother said.

Meg swallowed again, still not sure how to play this.

"I'm late," she said and ran down the hall, taking the

stairs to the first floor so fast that she almost fell. Her agents were waiting and she jumped into the car.

Wayne grinned at her. "Running a little late?"

"Yeah," Meg said. "Let's go."

"Trouble getting up?" Gary asked, starting the car.

"Let's just go, okay?" she said. "I mean, please."

She went straight to her locker when she got to school, not pausing to talk to anyone or even say hello. She opened it, not bothering to admire the decorations inside. Big-shot seniors always decorated their lockers. Hers had a mainly photographic motif. There was a bookstore on Connecticut Avenue where you could get really wild cards and she had postcards of old-time celebrities like Humphrey Bogart and Cary Grant. She also had pictures of people like Harrison Ford and anything she could find of Mel Gibson. There were postcards of Boston and one of Katharine Hepburn, but it was essentially a locker full of men. Usually, opening it cheered her up no matter what kind of mood she was in. Not today.

Alison wandered over. "Ready for the big match?" she asked cheerfully.

Meg shoved her racket into the locker. "Who cares about the stupid match."

Alison frowned. "What's with you?"

"Nothing."

"If you say so."

"I say so." Meg let her walk away, focusing on Cary Grant. Then, she sighed, feeling guilty. "Alison, wait."

Her friend turned. Alison qualified as a big-shot senior by the way she dressed: today she had on baggy gray corduroy pants, an Argyle sweater vest, an Oxford shirt that probably belonged to her brother Mark, and a loosely knotted silk tie. Annie Hall lives.

"I'm sorry." Meg kept her eyes on Cary Grant. "I guess I'm in a pretty lousy mood."

"I didn't notice."

Meg sighed, flipping her hair over her shoulders with a tired hand. "I'm sorry, I had a fight with my mother."

44

She was going to say, "my stupid mother," but it was tacky to be publicly derogative about parents.

"Um, a bad one?" Alison asked. People were usually cautious when they asked questions about the President.

"I'm probably grounded for the next *year.*" Meg searched through her knapsack for her English book and the essay she had spent half the night working on. The book wasn't there and she frowned, checking her locker.

"What's wrong?" Alison asked as she checked her knapsack again.

"I forgot my stupid English book." Because of my stupid mother. She gritted her teeth. You could *think* derogatory things about parents. "Mrs. Hayes is going to kill me."

"Just tell her you forgot it."

"Oh, yeah, great." Meg kicked her locker shut. "She'll probably flunk me."

"Not if you explain."

"Yeah, sure." Meg leaned against the locker for a second, resting her head on her arms. "You might want to stay away from me. I have a feeling I'm going to be mean to people."

She grumped her way through the morning, not participating in class, scrawling inane pictures in her notebook. Jagged lines, people skiing, Vanessa sleeping. People seemed to sense her mood and no one bugged her much, which made it easier not to offend anyone.

"Cheer up," Josh said as they walked into physics. "It can't be *that* bad."

"You weren't there," she said, taking her usual seat in the back. They always sat in the back.

"It's nothing to get worked up about," he said. "Everyone fights with their parents."

"Yeah." Meg twisted the spiral on her notebook. "But I was really a rat."

He shrugged. "They'll get over it. Just be really nice when you get home."

"Yeah, I guess."

"Hey, did you guys study for this?" Zachary asked.

Meg felt a nervous thump in her stomach. "Study for what?"

He grinned. "You're kidding, right?"

"N-no." She started to get scared. "Study for what?"

"We have that test today."

A test. Oh my God, we have a test. I forgot we had a test. Meg closed her eyes.

"You forgot?" Alison asked.

"Yeah."

"You have time." Josh opened her book for her. "It's just these formulas."

Meg looked at a page of completely unfamiliar material, then reclosed her eyes. What a day.

Her teacher came in right on time and handed out thick mimeographed exams that looked so difficult that even the people who had studied groaned.

She stared at incomprehensible motion and distance problems. She should have figured God would get her for being so rotten to everyone. Or maybe this was proof that there *was* no God.

She uncapped her pen, scribbling her name at the top of the sheet. The one good thing about physics was that you got partial credit. She looked at Josh who indicated that he would leave his paper in sight. She shook her head and he looked very relieved. But, as she struggled with the first problem, she couldn't help wishing for an act of God or a fire drill or something. That way, the test would be invalid.

Not getting anywhere, she glanced around and saw everyone else's pens and pencils moving. Terrific. She knew Josh would move his elbow for her, but she would never stoop to that. Pretty tempting though.

To avoid temptation, she picked up her pen. She shouldn't have been so rotten to everyone. So her parents wanted her to change out of her sweat pants, big deal. She should have just put on some jeans, and left it at that. But, no. Now the whole family was mad at her and she couldn't blame them.

Circumlocuting her way through the third problem, she

had a sudden, unexpected jolt of guilt, picturing her mother's expression. It was bad enough to be depressed yourself without ruining everyone else's day. Maybe she *deserved* to flunk this test.

There was a knock on the door as she tried to solve the eighth problem, panicking because she was running out of time. She didn't even look to see who was there and was surprised to hear her name.

"Meg," her teacher said again and she looked up. There was something strange in his expression as he gestured towards the door and she gulped without knowing why, a tight coldness starting in her neck and throat.

She stood up, clenching her pen hard enough to hurt her hand, and crossed to the door. Something's happened, I know something's happened. Please don't let anything have happened.

Her agents were standing in the hall, and feeling their concerned urgency, the coldness turned into a hard contraction of fear.

"Who is it?" she asked unsteadily.

"Your mother," one of them said.

CHAPTER SEVEN

Four shots had been fired. Maybe five. Her agents hustled her past the police barriers, past crowds of cameras, and into the hospital, which was gray and blue with Secret Service agents, white with doctors and nurses. Everyone was yelling at once.

She was steered into a small, noisy waiting room and scanned the faces through incredible dizziness, searching for her family. Neal jerked away from the aides who were holding him and she bent to hug him.

"Shh, it's okay," she whispered. "Don't worry, everything's okay."

He clutched her around the neck, crying so hard that his whole body shook.

"I know," she said, hugging him more tightly. "Don't worry, I'm here." She closed her eyes, afraid that she was going to cry too. But she had to be an adult. He needed an adult.

They were taken to another room, beige and windowless. Meg sat on a scuffed green leather couch, lifting her little brother onto her lap. The hall was a babble of tense, excited voices and she tried very hard not to listen, afraid of what she might hear.

"I'm scared," Neal whimpered, his arms tight enough to half-choke her.

"I know." She rubbed his back, struggling to be comforting. "Don't worry, it's going to be okay. I promise." She didn't look at anyone in the room, not wanting to see a contradiction in their expressions.

They sat, Meg holding and rocking him, whispering for him not to worry. Hearing noises at the door, she glanced up and saw Steven, looking as terrified as she felt, his hands tight fists in his pockets, his shoulders hunched up. Seeing her with Neal, his mouth quivered, but he didn't say anything, just came over and sat next to them on the couch.

"You okay?" she asked, not sure what else to say.

He didn't answer, his fists in his lap, arms rigid.

"Steven?"

He hunched more.

"Don't worry." She touched his shoulder. "It's going to be—"

"Leave me alone!" His voice was low, but definite.

She hesitated, then withdrew her hand after one gentle squeeze. An aide showed up with grape sodas, and to keep Neal occupied, she shared one with him, keeping up a steady monologue about how cold it was, how glad she was that it was Welch's because that was the only kind she liked and what did he think, and if he maybe wanted a sandwich or a Snickers bar. There was a lot of yelling in the hall and whenever there was a flurry of activity—people running in to whisper to aides who would then leave, any kind of shifting of personnel that might mean something bad—she spoke more loudly so they wouldn't have to pay attention to it. While the talking was distracting Neal, she could tell it was getting on Steven's nerves, but since he sat back at one point, still rigid, but at least not hunching, she figured it was helping.

No one seemed to know exactly what was happening, and the shouting in the hall was garbled. She would catch occasional phrases, when someone opened the door, but many of them seemed contradictory. All she really knew was what her agents had told her on the way over in the car, and that was pretty sketchy. "Shots fired, Shamrock hit. Transport Sandpiper." Shamrock was her mother's code name; Sandpiper was hers. All anyone knew for sure was that her mother *had* been hit, and that her father had been there when it happened. The two of them had been on the way to a luncheon of some kind and the shots had been fired from a second or third floor window when they got out of the car.

Her mother had been hit. And no one knew where. She closed her eyes, trying not to picture the bullet hitting her in the chest, or the head, or—she had to stop, had to pretend that none of this was happening, that—

"Meggie?" Neal asked, sounding scared.

"What?" She realized that she was trembling and must have unconsciously clutched at his arm. "I mean, don't worry, everything's okay." Maybe if she kept saying it, it would be true.

"I'm scared." He was crying again. "I want Mommy and Daddy."

"I know. Don't worry, they'll be here soon." She took a deep shaky breath. Now that she had started thinking, she couldn't stop remembering the things she had read in books and seen on television her whole life, all the people who had been shot, all the—except she couldn't. She couldn't let herself think about it, she had to stop picturing the shots, her mother falling, the blood—stop it! she ordered herself. Stop thinking about it. You want to crack up in front of Steven and Neal? Get a grip, damn it!

But, that beautiful gray dress. Her mother falling, the blood spreading over the gray cloth, agents swarming around—stop it! Kennedy, King, Kennedy, Wallace, Sadat—stop it! Stop thinking about it. Don't—something touched her arm and she stiffened, looking up to see Preston sitting on the table in front of the couch.

"Hey, kids," he said gently, one hand on Meg's shoulder, the other on Steven's, Neal in between them.

Looking at him, Meg got scared. He was—rumpled. Sleeves rolled up, tie undone, his handkerchief nowhere in sight. And he seemed tired. Very, very tired. She swallowed, knowing that her brothers were as afraid to ask him what was happening as she was.

"How are you kids doing?" he asked.

Meg gulped. "Is—I mean, is everything—"

"We're going to have to wait for a little while," he said.

"Is Mom—" Steven's voice was very small. "Is she—"

"There're a lot of people trying to help her. We just have to wait a little longer." He glanced at Meg. "We've got some lunch out there for you guys. How about giving me a hand, Meggo?"

She nodded, guessing that he wanted to speak to her privately, having to swallow several times at the thought.

"How come I can't come?" Steven asked. "Can't I—"

"No," Preston said. "Hang out here and keep Neal company."

Steven nodded unhappily and Preston hugged him, then Neal, as Meg stood up, finding her right leg asleep, but careful not to make a big production of stamping on it.

"Be right back, guys." Preston gestured for an aide to come sit with Steven and Neal, a woman by the door responding.

Meg followed him out to the crowded corridor, walking requiring a conscious, difficult effort.

"Are you okay, kid?" he asked.

She nodded, even though she wasn't.

"Good," he said. "Because you're going to have to keep taking care of them for a while. I don't know when your father's going to be able to get down here."

"Is Mom—" She swallowed. "What's happening?"

"They've been operating since noon," he said, automatically checking his watch.

"Is she—" Meg tried not to gulp visibly. "I mean, where—"

"The shoulder and the chest. And Bert Travis took one in the leg." Bert Travis was one of her mother's agents.

"So he'll be okay," Meg said, looking down at her hands.

Preston nodded.

"Mom—" She swallowed. "N-not the head?"

"No, kid," he said gently, putting his arm around her. "Not the head."

Meg blinked, not wanting him to see how close she was to crying. "I was mean to her this morning. I wouldn't—"

"Forget it," he said.

"But—"

"Forget it." He leaned over to kiss her forehead. "Can you handle your brothers for a while longer?"

She nodded. "When will Dad be able to come see us?"

Preston hesitated. "As soon as he can. He's in pretty bad shape."

"Should I—I mean, is there anything I can—"

"You can take care of your brothers," he said.

Back in the waiting room, she hid shaking hands in her pockets, aware that she was pretty obviously without lunch.

"The sandwiches weren't ready yet," she said.

Her brothers didn't say anything, waiting for older-sister answers.

"I guess it's going to be a while," she said and sat on the couch. "M-maybe they could bring in a television or something. We could—"

"I don't think we'll be able to find one," an aide interrupted, and she remembered what every station was probably showing. How many times had she watched live coverage—or historical footage—of shootings? How many times had she watched without ever thinking about the family that was falling apart somewhere? The films never showed the family.

They were in the room for a long time. Meg kept her arm around Neal, who cried on and off, finally falling asleep against her. Steven, who had been slouching down with his fists clenched, noticed, and sat up.

"Okay," he said in a low voice. "What's going on?"

"I told you," she answered, careful not to wake Neal up. "Everything's okay."

"Then how come Dad isn't here?"

She hesitated, not sure what to say.

"I'm not a little kid," he said. "What's going on?"

She looked at him, small and stiff, fists tight. "They're operating on her."

"Is she—I mean, where—"

"Not the head." She saw his eyes get very bright. "Steven, they're doing their—"

"Shut up!"

"Steven—"

52

"Just shut up!" He kicked the table as hard as he could, standing and kicking over a chair.

"Steven—"

"Shut up and leave me alone!"

"Meggie?" Neal woke up, clutching at her as she moved to get Steven. "Meggie, don't leave me!"

"I'm not." She tried to pry his hands off her arm. "Neal, I'm just—" She winced as Steven, who was crying now, kicked over another chair.

"Come on, Steve," an agent said, gently trying to stop him. "Calm down. Your mother's going to be—"

"Get off me!" Steven punched at him and the other agent who came over to help.

"Come on, son," the second agent said. "Let's—"

"I'm not your son!" Steven yelled. "Stupid jerks! You're supposed to protect her, you let them shoot her! You let them—"

"Steven, don't." Meg managed to pull away from Neal and get in between her brother and the agents. "Steven—"

"Leave me alone!" He kept swinging, hitting out at anything that came near him, kicking and struggling as an agent gently held him from behind, pinning one of his arms. "Let go of me!" He kept the other arm flailing. "Let go of me, you son of a bitch!" The fist got Meg in the face and she gasped before she could stop herself, her hand going to her mouth. He heard the gasp and went limp, staring at her, tears streaming down his cheeks.

"Meggie, I'm sorry." The agent let go of him and he stumbled forward against her. "I'm sorry, I didn't mean to. I didn't—"

"It's okay." She put her arms around him. "It isn't your fault. I walked into it."

"But I hit you. I didn't mean to. I really didn't mean to."

"I know. It's okay."

"Don't hate me! Please don't hate me!"

"I love you," she said.

"But—"

"I really do." She reached back to pull Neal over,

knowing that he must have been terrified by the scene. "I love both of you."

"Don't leave us again," Steven whispered, hanging on to her as tightly as Neal was. "Please?"

"I won't," she promised.

CHAPTER EIGHT

Once Steven started crying, he couldn't seem to stop, and he held her hand as they all sat on the couch. An aide *did* bring in sandwiches, but neither of her brothers would eat and Meg felt too sick at the thought of food to try to make them. There was something tiring about just sitting on a couch for hours and she concentrated on staying awake, the room windowless and stuffy.

"What time is it?" Neal asked sleepily.

Meg squinted at the nearest aide's watch. "Almost six." She kissed the side of his head. "You didn't have any lunch. You want one of those sandwiches maybe?"

He shook his head and she didn't push him. There was noise in the hall, the first sounds she'd heard after hours of ominous silence, and she leaned forward for one of the cans of warm grape soda, drinking some to steady herself. Her mother's aides were exchanging glances and Meg held her breath, perching on the edge of the couch, hearing a lot of low voices as one of the aides opened the door.

"What is it?" Steven asked. "Is something happening?"

"I don't know. I'll go find out." She followed the exodus of aides and agents to the hall, so dizzy that she wasn't sure she could walk. She met a grinning Preston on his way through to see them.

"It's okay, kid," he said. "She came through it okay."

Meg started to speak, then realized that she had to sit down. Quickly. She lowered herself into a chair while Preston continued over to her brothers. People were talking at her, but she didn't answer, too dizzy to even sit up straight.

"I know how you feel, kid," Preston said, by her chair suddenly.

Meg lifted her face out of her hands, managing to smile. "When can we see them?"

"I'm not sure. We're going to move the three of you upstairs though. At least get you on the same floor."

Preston and a bunch of agents led them through some offices, to a back hallway and staircase, up to the floor where the recovery room was. The new waiting room was more comfortable, with easy chairs and an overstuffed couch, and the three of them were finally allowed to be by themselves, away from all the aides and agents, although the room was heavily guarded.

"Your father will be down in a little while," Preston said, glancing at Meg. "In the meantime, can we get you guys anything?"

"Yeah," Steven said, his grin huge. "You got some food around this place?"

A lot of people stopped by to visit them in the next couple of hours—Vice-President Kruger and his wife, Cabinet members, the Speaker of the House, the Senate Majority Leader, all kinds of people. Meg did most of the talking while her brothers sat around and looked happy.

All she knew now was that their mother was "resting comfortably." Apparently, her condition was serious, but stable. Meg was very polite, making small talk with the visitors—none of whom stayed long—but she kept her eyes on the door, waiting for her father to come.

Right before eight, he did.

"Daddy!" Neal scrambled off the couch, running over to meet him.

Their father bent to hug him and Meg noticed that he was wearing a different outfit from the one he'd had on at breakfast. He was smiling, but his eyes were dark and his face had the look of newspaper someone had crumpled, then tried to smooth out again. His hands were shaking in a way that she usually associated with his having too much caffeine.

56

"I'm sorry," he said, hugging Steven now as Neal hung on to his jacket. "I had to be with your mother."

"Is she okay?" Steven asked. "She's going to be okay, right?"

Their father nodded, somewhat mechanically.

"Can we see her?" Neal asked.

"Probably in the morning," he said. "She's resting right now." He hugged Meg and she saw how bloodshot his eyes were, from strain probably, but it looked more as if he had been crying. She hugged him harder.

"I'm sorry," she said.

He nodded, and she could hear him swallow before he broke away.

"What I think you all ought to do," he said, "is go back to the house for the night."

"Why can't we stay here?" Steven asked. "They've got plenty of beds."

"Because there isn't anything you can do here," their father said. "And I'd feel better knowing that you were all at home and I didn't have to worry about you."

I wish I could stay, Meg thought. But if she asked, Steven and Neal would have a fit. She looked from her father, to the agents he was instructing, to her hands. Maybe she could go with her brothers and then come back, or maybe—

"Aren't you coming too?" Neal asked their father.

"I'll probably be spending the night," he said. "You all can come back in the morning when your mother's feeling better."

When her brothers were distracted for a minute, Meg moved closer to her father. "Do I have to go?" she asked.

"It would be a lot easier," he said, looking at Steven and Neal.

She nodded, careful not to seem reluctant.

He put his hand on her shoulder. "I know how you feel. But right now, the important thing for you to do is to take care of your brothers."

She nodded.

"I'm counting on you."

She nodded.

The White House was somber. Somber and solicitous, everyone waiting on them hand and foot. Meg got her brothers settled in the West Sitting Hall, butlers bringing them things like chocolate milkshakes and brownies, and once her brothers were eating, she went down to her room so she could be alone.

Vanessa was asleep on the bottom of her bed and Meg picked her up, hugging her to her chest, comforted by the warm purring. She hugged her closer, not wanting to start crying. Once she felt under control, she opened her eyes, sitting up straighter. Vanessa flexed her paws, digging them into Meg's chamois shirt, and Meg extricated them, looking at the delicate shape of her cat's leg, soft gray fading into white, with tiny clean claws and barely scarred pads. The white and gray made her think of her mother's dress, that beautiful flannel pinstripe. She pictured her mother getting out of the car; tall, thin, elegant. Maybe wearing a gray wool coat, but probably not since it was only October. Smiling at the crowd—there was always a crowd—and then—then—

"Meggie?" Steven asked from the door.

She sat all the way up, releasing Vanessa. "What?"

"Will you come watch TV with us?"

"What's on?" she asked cautiously.

"I don't know, some stupid movie." He shifted his weight. "Please, Meggie?"

She nodded and they went to the solarium, Steven and Neal sitting on either side of her on the couch. The movie turned out to be a police drama that might have violence, so she put on a situation comedy that they hated. There was a news update right before the show started, and she had to turn the channel swiftly, before her brothers could hear anything more than "Tonight Presi—" As soon as she figured it was safe, she turned back and they watched the comedy, none of them laughing. After that, a night-time soap opera came on and they sat through half of that.

"I'm tired," Neal said.

"Yeah, you should get some sleep," she agreed.

"Will you come with me?"

"Sure." She looked at Steven. "Will you be okay up here?"

"I'm coming too," he said.

They went down to the second floor and Meg sent them into their bedrooms to put on their pajamas.

"May we bring you anything?" Felix asked as she stood in the West Sitting Hall.

"No, thank you. I'm fine."

"I hope you know how sorry all of us are," he said.

She nodded. "Thank you."

"There are a lot of phone messages, including—"

She shook her head. "I'll look at them in the morning. I'm too tired to think right now."

He nodded. "I'll have them put on your night table."

"Thank you."

"Mrs. Donovan called to say that she would be on the next plane up here."

Meg looked up. "Really? Do you think she'll get here tonight?"

"I know she's going to try."

"I hope so." Mrs. Donovan was Trudy, who, until they came to the White House, had been their housekeeper for practically Meg's entire life. She had become more of a grandmother than anything else, the only grandparent kind of person they had. When they moved to the White House, she had gone to Florida to live near her son, who had four-year-old twins. Meg hadn't seen her since July when she had come to stay for two weeks, which had been wonderful. Almost like being home.

Neal came out of his bedroom, wearing light blue pajamas.

"Did you brush your teeth?" Meg asked.

"No."

"Go brush your teeth. Then, I'll come in and keep you company."

He nodded, leaving as Steven appeared, wearing old gray sweat pants and a long underwear shirt.

"Did you brush your teeth?" Meg asked.

He made a face and sat down at the shiny wooden table where her parents ate breakfast on Sunday mornings and read *The Times*.

"Felix says Trudy called and she's coming," Meg said.

"Tonight?"

"I don't know. If she can. It's kind of late."

"Meg?" Neal called from his bedroom.

"Be right there," she called back. She glanced at Steven. "I said I'd keep him company for a while."

He nodded, following her.

Neal was sitting on his bed and Meg helped him under the covers, tucking him in, then sitting on the edge of the bed as Steven slouched into an armchair. Seeing how tired Neal's eyes were, she turned off his light, then took his hand.

"Will we see Mommy tomorrow?" he asked.

She nodded. "In the morning."

"Will she come home then?"

"I don't know. Probably not tomorrow, but soon."

"Is she thinking about us?"

"Of course." She could see his smile in the light from the hall and patted his cheek with her free hand. "Trudy's coming too."

"Is she here now?"

"We'll see her tomorrow too."

"Will she stay and take care of us?"

"Yeah."

He smiled and closed his eyes, and she sat there until she was sure he was asleep. Then, after a few more minutes, she extricated her hand from his and stood up, straightening his blankets, then turning to see what Steven was doing.

He was almost asleep himself and she very gently shook his shoulder, taking him to his room and doing as much tucking in as his thirteen-year-old pride would allow. Satisfied that he was okay, she went out to the hall. Kirby was asleep in front of her parents' bedroom door and she patted him, then brought him into Steven's room, Kirby jumping onto the bed and settling himself, with the awkwardness of large dogs, on Steven's legs.

Deciding that Neal needed an animal too, she wandered around the second floor until she found Humphrey, their tiger cat, in the Queen's Bedroom and carried him down to Neal's room, depositing him on the bed.

The house was very quiet. The West Wing was probably full of activity—Vice-President Kruger and aides working through the night—but in the West Sitting Hall, she felt as if she were the only person in the entire building. Lonely, but not tired enough to go to bed yet, she sat on a couch, not sure what to do.

"Miss Powers?"

She flinched, then saw that it was only Felix. "Um, yes?"

"There's a phone call for you—Miss Shulman calling from Boston. Would you like to take it?"

Beth. "Very much," Meg said.

"Shall I have it transferred to your room or—?"

"No." Meg indicated the Presidential Bedroom. "I'll take it in there." She stood up. "Thanks."

The room seemed strange and empty without her parents and, once inside, Meg regretted not having the call transferred to her own room. But the phone was already ringing and she would feel stupid asking them to transfer it *again*. She was going to pick up the phone next to her mother's side of the bed, but that seemed wrong, so she picked up the one on her desk.

"Hello?" she said automatically.

"Are you all right?" Beth asked.

Hearing her voice, Meg relaxed into the chair, coming—for the first time—very close to bursting into tears. "Hi."

"Are you okay?"

Meg slouched lower, pressing her hand across her eyes so she wouldn't cry. "Yeah."

"Is this an okay time for you to talk?"

"Yeah."

"I'm sorry. I mean—I'm *really* sorry."

Meg nodded, forgetting that Beth was several hundred miles away and couldn't see her.

"How is she?"

Meg swallowed. "Pretty bad. I mean, we weren't allowed to see her or anything."

"Tomorrow?"

"I guess." Feeling cold, Meg hunched into her shirt. "I don't know."

"You sound terrible."

"I'm just tired."

"You want me to call you back tomorrow?"

"No. I mean—" Meg sighed. "I don't know."

"You should sleep."

"I can't *sleep*. I mean—Christ. I can't—I don't know."

"Is anyone there?"

"No, Dad's at the hospital. I mean, Steven and Neal are here, but—" Meg let out her breath, too tired to finish the sentence. "I don't know."

"Is there anything I can do?"

"No. I mean, thanks, but—no."

"You should go sleep. If you're tired, things'll be even harder."

"Yeah, probably."

"I really am sorry, Meg. I wish—there isn't anything I can do?"

"No, not really."

"Why don't you go to bed and I'll call you tomorrow?"

Meg nodded, rubbing her sleeve across her face. "I mean, yeah," she said aloud.

"Is there a good time to call?"

"Wait," Meg shook her head. "Maybe I should call *you*. It'd be easier."

"Okay, whatever." Beth paused. "Call anytime. I mean, even later tonight if you want. I'll just unplug the extension in my mother's room."

Meg nodded sleepily.

"Get some sleep, okay?"

"Yeah," Meg agreed. "Thanks for calling." After hanging up, she stayed at the desk for a few minutes, leaning forward with her head on her arms. Weird—spooky, almost—to have a conversation with Beth during which neither one of them made jokes. Especially Beth, who took great pride in *never* being serious. Except all of this was pretty damn serious.

She sat up and looked around the room. Her parents' room. It was large and impressive, but somehow cozy. That is, when her parents were there. They would always have a fire going and the whole family would watch television instead of going to the solarium or to their rooms. Tonight, it didn't seem cozy at all.

Her mother usually sat at the desk, going through papers until she was tired, then moving to the bed where Neal and Meg's father would be, Meg's father reading as well as watching television. Steven would be in an easy chair or lying on the carpet, and Meg would sit on the couch, holding homework on her lap so her parents would think she was doing it. Every now and then, she would even complete a physics problem or a French exercise. Felix, or whoever was on duty, generally brought in popcorn. Of course, lots of nights, her parents would be out at political things, or there would be dinners and receptions downstairs. There were always foreign dignitaries, astronauts, or movie stars to honor. Meg hated wearing evening gowns, but if exciting people were coming, she would usually go, with Josh as her escort. Sometimes directors and actors came to screen their movies in the theater downstairs, and Meg *always* went to those. Even if there weren't any actors around, they could get movies whenever they wanted. Sort of a fringe benefit.

Her parents' Siamese cats, Adlai and Sidney, were asleep on the bed and she walked over to pat them. There were books and magazines on both bedside tables and Meg thought about coming in when her parents were getting ready to go to bed, lying down, each reading a novel. Her mother always set aside some time, right before going to sleep, to relax with fiction for a while. It was probably the only relaxation she ever got. She wasn't very good at lounging around and doing nothing—although Meg had offered to give her lessons—and when she played tennis or skied, she was usually so competitive and self-demanding that it couldn't really be described as relaxation.

Meg remembered coming into the bedroom once, early on a Saturday morning, and finding her mother sitting on the couch in a gray skirt and silk shirt, hands folded in her lap. "What are you doing?" Meg asked. Her mother frowned and said, "Nothing." Meg looked at the paper-crowded desk, the morning newspapers everywhere, the untouched cup of coffee. "Aren't you going to have breakfast?" she asked, very hungry. "I don't feel like it," her mother said, then frowned again. "I don't really feel like doing anything." "So don't," Meg shrugged. Her mother just frowned, put on her reading glasses—which meant that she hadn't even bothered to put in her contacts yet—picked up a morning briefing report and started reading, comparing the news summary with the highlighted early editions of *The Times* and *The Post*. Watching her, Meg wondered if people knew that sometimes her mother wasn't in the mood to be President. Were all Presidents like that? All world leaders? Surely everyone woke up sometimes and felt like being anything *but* in charge.

Seeing how unhappy her mother looked, Meg sat down and started an inane conversation. Her mother seemed annoyed, then amused, putting her papers down, taking off the glasses, and they sat for about fifteen minutes, talking about nothing in particular, her mother slowly relaxing. Then, a butler arrived with a tray of breakfast—more coffee, hot scones, butter, jams, fresh fruit. The phone started ringing with requests from aides, questions from the press staff, and about nine thousand other things, and Meg watched her mother turn into the President again. She remembered finding the whole incident depressing, wondering if her mother enjoyed her life or just put up with it. There were definitely days when the latter seemed true.

Like today. Except that today must be a day that she *hated* the Presidency. Meg sure did. In fact, she kind of hated the entire country. How could you not hate a country where Presidents who were only trying to do good things were shot just for getting out of a car?

It was almost eleven-thirty. "Nightline" was always on, but on days when bad things happened, all three networks usually had a special on, explaining the day's events. Tonight was probably one of those nights.

She stared at the blank television screen, a pale, translucent gray. There was something frightening about television screens—one flick of a switch and they would burst to life, giving you the feeling that they had been alive all along and—she was afraid to bring today to life. Only, which was worse—imagining what had happened, or actually seeing it? The shots, the shouts, the blood—maybe imagining was worse.

She turned the television on. "Nightline" was on and she stepped back, arms tight across her chest.

"—yet another in a long series of violent—"

Meg closed her eyes. She shouldn't be watching this. Talk about masochistic. She had seen most of the tragedies of the last decade on instant replay. The reaction to a shooting was, "Oh, again?" There were probably people all over the country watching this, clicking their tongues, then switching over to see what was on HBO. She had probably done it herself; shootings seemed both distant and commonplace.

The reporter was describing the scene at the downtown Washington hotel and Meg frowned, staring at it. It was almost always a hotel. The last time one of these things had happened to a President, it had been a hotel. Why had the stupid Secret Service let her mother go to a hotel?

"—at the top left corner of your screen is the window where Bruce Sampson was waiting—"

Meg opened her eyes, staring at the harmless, venetian-blinded window, open about four inches.

"—the thirty-six-year-old unemployed Sampson had a history of—"

Meg flinched as the photograph of a surly, thick-necked man came onto the screen.

"—previous convictions include assault with a deadly weapon, assault with intent to kill, and various sexual—"

Not wanting to hear any more of that, the trembling spreading up through her back and shoulders, Meg switched to another channel and saw the presidential motorcade pulling up to the hotel.

"At exactly eleven-thirteen, the President stepped out of her limousine, surrounded by—"

Meg gulped, seeing her mother get out of the car, agents everywhere as she smiled at the press and onlookers, staff members from the other cars joining the group around her. The film was a little shaky, the cameraperson jostling for position maybe. Her mother turned slightly as her father got out of the car and the first shot turned her even more, the sound like a small firecracker. The film was confusing: a blur of blue and gray agents, but the audio stayed on and Meg heard all of the shouting she had imagined—worse than she had imagined—along with three more shots. She couldn't see her parents, but agents were piling into the presidential limousine, which swerved away from the sidewalk, most of the motorcade right behind it.

She watched the pandemonium of the aftermath, shaking too hard to move or look away. People were shouting and yelling; agents were clustered around Bert Travis, the agent who had been hit in the leg; still more agents were tearing across the street to the building from which the shots had come. She reached her hand over to the television, shaking almost convulsively, and switched the set off, the room instantly dark, silent except for her own breathing.

Someone had shot her mother. Someone had actually—that man had taken a gun and—Meg leaned against her mother's desk, her legs feeling weak. Except that she was supposed to be in charge. Instead of sitting around and being upset, she should go check her brothers and make sure they were sleeping. She took one steadying breath and pushed away from the desk, going to Neal's room first. His blankets were rumpled, but he didn't seem too restless, so she retucked him in and went to make sure that Steven was okay.

Opening the door to his room, she heard quiet crying. She shouldn't have waited so long to go check on them. He was on his stomach, face pressed into his long-underwear sleeve, crying, his other arm around Kirby. She sat down on the bed, rubbing his back.

"It's okay," she said. "Don't worry, it's okay."

"I'm scared," he said, trying to stop crying.

"Don't be, everything's okay."

"What if," he gulped, "what if she—" He took a shuddering breath. "What if she dies?"

Meg had to gulp too. "She's not going to."

"But what if she does?"

"She won't."

"But what if she *does?*" He turned over, his face so flushed that she was afraid he was sick. "What if that's why they sent us home?"

Meg didn't answer right away, the fear sounding very plausible, one that she had been worrying about inside too. Not that she could tell *him* that. "Look," she made up a quick rebuttal, "if they thought something was going to happen, they would have *kept* us there."

"How do you know?"

She fell back on her most irrefutable answer. "I'm older than you are."

He sat up, arms going around his knees. "Dad looked like he'd been crying. Do you think he was?"

Yes. "I think it's just because he was tired," she said.

"I've never seen him crying," Steven said uneasily. "Have you?"

"No."

"He looked scared too." Steven's eyes were huge. "I didn't know he got scared. I didn't think he ever got afraid."

Meg moved her jaw. What could she say to that? "I don't know."

Steven crunched himself up more. "It makes me scared too," he said and she leaned forward to brush hair—damp from tears, perspiration, or both—away from his forehead, both of them quiet.

"If, uh, you want, you can go to bed," he said finally.

"Do you want me to?"

He shrugged his "I'm thirteen, I'm cool" shrug, even though his eyes were still bright with tears.

"I could bring a cot in here," she suggested.

"I dunno. If you're lonely or something, you can."

She had to smile. "I'm lonely," she said.

CHAPTER NINE

They went to the hospital at nine-thirty, Secret Service cars driving both in front of and behind them, a crowd of agents escorting them inside, more security than Meg had ever seen. It was scary, as if they were all expecting a crowd of machine-gun-carrying guerrillas to show up.

Preston met them in the waiting room.

"Your mother's feeling much better," he said. "You'll be able to go in and see her for a minute."

"When?" Steven asked, neat in a striped tie and his navy blue blazer. Neal was also wearing a tie and Meg had put on a skirt.

"In just a little while." Preston reached down to take Neal's hand. "We're going to wait for your father."

"Where is he?" Steven asked, suspicious.

"Finishing shaving."

Steven frowned, not convinced, and stood at the door to wait.

"Late night?" Meg asked in a low voice.

"*All* night," Preston said, just as low.

"Is he—okay?"

"Try to get him to eat with all of you. If he goes much longer, he's going to collapse."

Meg nodded, feeling her fists tighten nervously. Preston also nodded, patting her shoulder.

A few minutes later, her father came in with a crowd of agents. He had shaved and changed his clothes, but he looked terrible, gray and exhausted. And drained. Preston was right about them getting him to eat. He hugged each of them, hanging on longer than usual.

"How's Mommy?" Neal asked.

"Better," their father said. "We're going to go down

and see her." He turned to Preston. "Do me a favor and clear the room, will you? And make sure no one's going to bother us on the way down."

Preston nodded, crossing to the aides standing on the other side of the room. A few quiet words and they all left, Preston following them to the corridor.

"Is she *really* okay?" Steven asked.

"Well," their father spoke carefully, sitting on the couch with Neal on his lap, "you have to remember that she's hurt. She's not going to be sitting up or walking around."

"Will she be awake?" Steven's scared expression was back.

"Yes. But," their father hugged Neal closer, "we all have to be very gentle. We're only going to stay in there for a minute and then we're going to leave so she can get some rest. We don't want to make her talk either. She has some tubes to help her breathe and it hurts her throat to talk."

"D-does she look like TV?" Neal asked.

"She looks like your mother," their father said. "Don't worry." He reached over to touch Meg's face, resting his hand on her cheek. "You too."

Meg nodded. Did Steven want to be young enough to sit on her father's lap and be comforted as much as she did?

Their father stood up, holding Neal's hand. "Why don't we go down there?"

Meg wanted to stay close to him too, to have him rest his hand on her shoulder or back, but since Steven was brave enough to stand alone, hands jammed into his pockets, then she, as the oldest, should be too.

Her mother's room was large and full of doctors and nurses. Meg made herself look again, more calmly, and saw that there were only six. Only six. She followed her father and brothers to the bed, hearing the various hums and bleeps of medical machines, afraid to see what her mother looked like.

"Hi, Mom," she heard Steven say, his voice choking.

"Mommy." Neal's voice was higher, but just as scared.

Come on, look up. You have to look up. Meg lifted her head and saw her mother, pale and fragile, her right arm full of tubes, more tubes going through her nose and down her throat. The bed had been propped up to make it seem as if she were sitting, but she was obviously very weak. Her left arm was in a sling, tightly bandaged near her shoulder and neck, and there were more bandages visible through the hospital gown, her whole upper body bulky. Incredibly, she was smiling. A trembling smile, but one that stayed on.

Say something. You have to say something. "Hi." Meg's voice didn't come out right and she tried again. "H-hi. How are you feeling?"

"Fine." Her mother's voice also rasped, but that was because of the tubes.

"Katie," Meg's father said, gently warning, and Meg saw her mother's eyes glisten as she nodded.

She glanced to see what her brothers were doing. Neal was hanging on to their father's hand, staring at their mother, and Steven had his fists in his pockets, so expressionless that Meg had to look twice before she realized that he was crying. No one spoke.

"Um," one of the doctors said, "I think—"

"We just got here!" Meg blinked, surprised by the anger in her own voice.

"He's probably right," her father said. "The more rest your mother gets, the sooner she'll be able to come home. Come on." He lifted Neal up. "Let's all give your mother a kiss so she'll be able to sleep better."

"Will it hurt you?" Neal asked her, uneasy.

Her mother shook her head and weakly snapped the fingers of her right hand, Meg's father moving a legal pad over, along with a Magic Marker. "It will make me feel *better*," she wrote in shaky but distinguishable handwriting.

Neal kissed her cheek, pulling away fast.

"Good job," her mother wrote. "My arm just healed." She winked at him and he giggled, Meg staring at her in frank admiration. Steven moved close enough to kiss her, wiping his blazer sleeve across his eyes to get rid of some of the tears. Their mother brought her hand over to his face, holding it there, and he burst into even harder tears.

"I hate him," he said, then ran out of the room.

"Steven," her mother tried to call after him, her voice sounding terrible.

"I'll take care of it," Meg's father said. He bent to kiss her cheek and whispered something, her mother nodding. "Come on," he said to Meg and Neal, standing up.

"C-can I—" Meg swallowed. "I mean, just for a minute?"

He looked at the doctors, then nodded. "Just for a minute."

When he and Neal were gone, she looked at her mother. "I, uh, I'm sorry."

Her mother nodded and wrote, "I'm sorry for all of us."

"Do you hurt?"

Her mother shook her head. "How are your brothers?" she wrote.

"Okay," Meg said. "Steven's having a harder time."

Her mother nodded. "What about you?" she wrote.

Meg started to say that she was fine, but instead, began crying. Her mother reached out to take her hand, holding on with surprising strength. Meg hung on tightly, knowing that she had to be a little kid for a minute, let someone else be the strong one. But it didn't seem right to be *taking* strength from someone she should be giving it to, so she let go, getting herself under control with a deep, shaky breath.

"Meg," her mother said hoarsely. "It's okay to—"

"Madame President." One of the doctors indicated his throat.

72

Her mother looked annoyed, but pulled over her legal pad, turning to a fresh page. "Let yourself get upset," she wrote. "Don't try to hold it in."

"I'm fine," Meg said.

Her mother looked at her and Meg felt even more power from the gaze than she had felt from her mother's hand. She wouldn't have looked away, but a nurse tapped her shoulder, gesturing towards the door.

"I have to go," Meg said. "I mean, they want me to."

Her mother nodded, most of the power fading from her eyes, something like vulnerability or loneliness replacing it.

"I'll be back as soon as they let me." Meg bent down, not wanting the doctors and nurses to overhear her. "I really love you," she whispered, kissed her mother's cheek and swiftly left the room. Remembering that she had been crying, she wiped away the last of the tears with her hand, and agents escorted her down to the waiting room where her father and brothers were, all three looking up as she came in, Steven's face tear-stained.

"Hi," Meg said and sat in an empty chair, very tired. She hadn't gotten very much sleep. Felix had helped her get a cot into Steven's room and once she was settled, unaccountably cold and huddling under two blankets, Steven had fallen asleep and she was the one lying alone and scared in the darkness. Even holding Vanessa hadn't helped. It must have been almost dawn by the time she had finally fallen asleep because she remembered watching the sky change colors through Steven's window.

She leaned her head against the hard vinyl back of the chair, studying the ceiling. People in the room were talking, maybe even to her, but she concentrated on the ceiling, too tired to follow a conversation. The fluorescent lights hurt her eyes, so she closed them, not wanting to get a worse headache than the one she had. It was nice to rest for a minute. Just for a minute.

A hand touched her shoulder and she opened her eyes, jumping when she saw Josh sitting in a chair next to the couch. Meg stared at him in confusion, not sure where they were or why she was lying on the couch with a blanket over her and just the two of them in the room.

"I'm sorry, I didn't mean to wake you up," he said. "You were having a bad dream."

She squinted at him, still confused. "Josh?"

"Hi," he said, with such a nice, gentle smile that she decided that this *was* Josh and she *was* awake. "Are you all right?"

"Um—" Her face felt damp and she realized that she must have been crying in her sleep. She turned away, embarrassed, wiping the tears with her hand.

"You okay?"

"What?" Meg shook her head, trying to get rid of the last of the confusion. "I mean, what are you doing here?"

"Well, I just—I mean, I thought you might—"

"Don't we have school?"

"Yeah. I, uh," he looked sheepish, "kind of didn't go."

"To come here?"

"Yeah." He leaned forward, brushing the hair away from her face.

"What time is it?"

"Going on to two." He kept stroking her forehead and she was so tired that she sank down onto the pillow, letting him do it.

"Have you been here a long time?"

He shook his head. "They wouldn't let me in. Then, when Preston got back from the White House, he said it was okay."

Meg frowned, confused again. "Preston left?"

"Trudy got here and they took Steven and Neal home."

"Oh." She blinked hard, trying to force her eyes to stay open. "Is my father here?"

Josh nodded. "He's in with your mother."

"Oh." She let her eyes close.

"You want to sleep some more?"
She did, but she shook her head.
"You want a hug?"
Now, she opened her eyes. "Yeah," she said. "I do."

CHAPTER TEN

She stayed in his arms for what seemed like a long time.

"You should go home and sleep," he said softly.

Meg shook her head. She didn't want to leave without seeing her mother again.

"You'd feel better," he said.

"No, I wouldn't."

He started to disagree, then nodded. Meg also nodded, too tired to explain.

Preston came back, and sat with them for a while, and her father was in and out, but none of them talked much. Then, right before six, she got in to see her mother, this time for about ten minutes. The doctors had taken the throat tubes out and she was able to speak, making small-voiced jokes and being so damn game that Meg had to struggle not to cry, especially when her face would get gray and tight with pain and she would still try to make jokes.

After that, her father made her leave, six agents moving to accompany her.

"You want me to come?" Josh asked.

She wanted to go home and sleep, but couldn't figure out how to say so without being rude, so she nodded. The agents steered them out through a side exit, but there was still a crowd outside. Policemen, National Guard people, Secret Service, reporters, cameras going like crazy, protestors—*protestors?*—National Rifle Association, anti–National Rifle Association, yelling for her mother, against her mother—Meg stopped, too scared to go out there. She turned to go back inside, but there seemed to be even more people behind her, and she stopped again, completely terrified. Josh seemed to be saying something, but her heart was pounding too loudly for her to hear, and suddenly an agent was holding her arm, moving her through the crowd and into a black car, Josh jumping in right behind her. Then, the car was pulling away from the curb and she sank back against the seat, covering her face with her hands.

"You okay?" Josh asked, sounding very worried.

She nodded, tears too close to trust her voice. His hand was on her shoulder and she shook it off, leaning forward with her face still in her hands, trying to get control of herself.

"Meg—"

She shook her head, moving further away from him, concentrating on taking slow, calming breaths. Then, they were at the White House and she hurried out of the car, heading straight for the elevator upstairs, Josh behind her.

As he reached out to take her hand, she shook her head. "Just—don't, okay?"

He withdrew, putting his hands uncomfortably in his pockets. She knew it was probably because she was tired and upset, but there was something so annoying about the way he was standing that she had to concentrate on not looking at him. He must have felt something in the air because he shifted his weight, looking even more uncomfortable.

It was very quiet upstairs.

"Meg," he started.

"I think I hear people in the kitchen," she said, moving past him and down the hall.

Steven and Neal were sitting at the table, with glasses of milk instead of their usual Cokes, while Trudy stood at the stove, stirring things in various pots. Seeing her there, wearing a familiar blue flowered dress with an apron over it, bustling about, Meg leaned against the doorjamb, feeling—for a second—as if they were home and none of this White House stuff had ever happened.

"Meg's here," Steven said and Trudy turned, crossing the room to hug her.

"Uh, you remember Josh, don't you?" Meg said before she could do so.

"Of course," Trudy said. "How are you, Josh?"

He coughed. "Fine, ma'am."

She gave Meg a little squeeze, almost a hug, and Meg inhaled a couple of times. Trudy always smelled so good. Like sachets, and Certs, and talcum powder. As if she had just eaten a gumdrop.

"Why don't you two sit down with the boys?" she suggested, pulling away. "I'm just getting dinner ready."

"What are you making?" Meg asked, even though she wasn't hungry.

"That hamburger casserole all of you like."

Meg nodded. It was one of the few casseroles all of them *did* like, and they had had it many times over the years. Her head hurt suddenly, and she rubbed her hand across her forehead. All she wanted to do was go down to her room, get into bed, and turn off the lights. She should just tell Josh that she wanted to be alone and—except that she felt so shaky that she was either going to yell at him or burst into tears.

"Meg?" Trudy said. "Why don't you sit down?"

"No, I—" Control. She didn't want to lose control. But, all of a sudden, she felt—"Um, I'll be right back, okay?" She pushed past Josh and out to the West Sitting Hall, walking quickly—almost running—down to her room.

She was going to cry. She was very definitely going to cry. But she didn't want—she headed straight into the bathroom, turning on the cold water full blast, washing her face once, then again. It didn't help and she closed her eyes, gripping the sides of the sink with her hands. Control. She had to keep—she bit the inside of her cheek, increasing the pressure to keep the tears back. The man aiming the gun, the bullets ripping—she hung on to the sink more tightly. If he had aimed a little higher, or two inches to the left, her mother would be lying in the rotunda at the Capitol Building, and they would all have to be brave and follow the riderless horse to Arlington National Cemetery while—stop it! She had to stop it. Josh was here and she couldn't—she should have told him to go home, and—why hadn't she told him to go home?

She sat down, pressing her face into the cold washcloth, counting to ten. To thirty. Okay, okay. She was okay. Except she couldn't stop thinking about the man, waiting at the window, while she sat in physics, wishing for something, *anything*, to—she had to stop this. She couldn't keep—*thirty-one, thirty two*—she stopped at fifty, under control again.

They were all waiting for her in the kitchen—she had to go out there. Slowly, she rewashed her face, then went out to her room, pausing to lift Vanessa up for a quick cuddle. Then, she walked out to the hall, so tired that her arms and legs felt heavy.

Josh was sitting on one of the couches, waiting for her, and she stopped, not sure where the anger had come from, but suddenly furious.

"What are you doing," she asked, "following me?"

"No, I—"

"I *said* I'd be *right back.*"

"I know. I just—" He blinked—"wanted to be sure you were okay."

"Of course I'm not okay! Christ, would you be?"

"No, I—"

"Yeah, well, I just wanted to be alone—Christ, don't you understand *anything?*"

"I'm sorry," he said.

"Sorry? What good is sorry?" She rubbed her forehead, the ache much worse. "Just leave me alone."

He nodded, edging towards the stairs. "I'm sorry, I—"

"Stop saying that!"

He nodded. "Y-you want me to call you later?"

"No, I want you to leave me alone! Are you deaf or something?"

"No, I—I hope you feel better," he said.

"I'm not the one who's sick! I mean, hurt. I mean—" She turned away, walking back to her room. "Just leave me alone."

She stood inside her room, fists tightly clenched, trembling and out of breath. Some kind of angry energy came bubbling up and she kicked the side of her bookcase as hard as she could, several books flying out. Vanessa woke up, startled, and ran out of the room. Meg grabbed a book, wanting to throw it after her, but controlled the impulse, throwing it at the bathroom door instead. The book slammed against the wood, bouncing back onto the floor.

"Stupid cat." She kicked two of the books out of the way, walking over to the bed.

"Meg?" Steven asked, behind her.

She spun around. "Don't you knock? Jesus!"

"I'm sorry." He took a step backwards. "I was just—"

"Leave me alone, okay?"

He didn't move, staring at her.

"Okay?"

"Yeah, sure. Anything you say." He left, slamming the door on the way.

Finally alone, Meg climbed into bed, pausing only to take off her shoes. She turned off the light, then burrowed down under the covers, trembling from anger or fear or— someone knocked on the door.

She sat up, the anger back, full force. "I said, leave me alone!"

"Meg, it's me," Trudy said.

Oh, God. Meg slumped back down. "I need to be alone for a while," she said, more quietly.

"Are you all right?"

"Yeah. I just need to be alone."

"Call me if you need me."

"Yeah." Meg held her breath until she was sure Trudy was gone, then relaxed. Still shaking, she wrapped the blankets around herself and huddled down. She closed her eyes, fairly sure that she was going to cry, but fell asleep first.

When she woke up, it was very hot and she wondered if she were sick or—maybe it was just the blankets. She untwisted them, sitting up and looking at her clock, the red numbers blurry in the darkness. Ten-thirty. She slouched back down, staring at the ceiling. Sometimes, when you were upset, sleeping for a while made you feel better. Not this time. Her stomach hurt, but she wasn't sure if it was hunger or real pain. When was the last time she had eaten? Breakfast. Part of a bowl of Special K. No wonder she felt lousy.

She felt too sick to get up, so she rolled over onto her side, watching the red numbers on her clock change. She was just falling asleep when the phone rang. The hospital. What if something—she grabbed the receiver.

"Hello?"

"Miss Shulman for you," the switchboard person said. "Shall I put the call through?"

Meg sighed. "Yeah, I guess. I mean—yeah. Thanks."

Beth came on. "Meg?"

She sighed again. "Yeah."

"How is everything?"

Jesus *Christ,* she was tired of that question. "Terrible, how do you think?"

"That's what I figured."

"What do you mean, 'you figured'?" Meg asked, irritated. "Whad do *you* know about it?"

"Feeling kind of crummy tonight, huh?" Beth said.

Meg gritted her teeth. "I don't want to talk about it."

"Okay, no problem. You want me to hang up?"

"Yes."

"Okay, no problem." Beth paused. "Look, I was thinking. You want me to come down next week or something?"

Meg automatically moved the receiver away from her ear, looking at it. "Come *here?*" she asked, bringing the receiver back. "What do you mean?"

"I don't know. You sound like you need some company maybe."

"I don't," Meg said.

"We can just hang out, watch some movies, eat some food—you know."

"Beth, I really don't—" Meg let out her breath. "This isn't a very good time, know what I mean?"

"Hmmm," Beth said. "Not exactly hospitable, are you?"

Meg was going to yell at her, but found her face relaxing instead. "Has anyone ever told you what a jerk you are?"

"Just about everyone," Beth said.

"Yeah, well—" Meg sighed. "Put me at the top of the list."

"Sure," Beth promised. "So. Can I come?"

"Jesus, Beth."

"Well, think about it, okay? I can just get on that shuttle."

"Yeah. I don't know." Meg slouched down in bed, aware that her headache was back, worse than ever. "I'll see what happens."

"Okay. I'm going to hang up," Beth said. "I hope you feel better."

"I'm not sick!"

"You know what I mean. Take it easy, okay?"

"Oh, yeah," Meg said. "Absolutely."

After hanging up, she lay in bed, staring up at the ceiling, carefully *not* thinking.

There was a quiet knock on the door. "Meg?"

Trudy. "What." She shook her head. She shouldn't be rude to Trudy. She was never rude to Trudy. "I mean, come in."

Trudy opened the door, carrying a tray into the room. "I thought you might be hungry."

"Oh." Meg sat up, managing to smile instead of saying that her stomach hurt and she would rather be left alone. "I mean, thank you."

Trudy put the tray on her lap: vegetable soup, a grilled cheese sandwich cut in triangles—Trudy was big on bread triangles—a dish of chocolate-chip ice cream, a glass of milk.

"Um, thank you," Meg said. "It looks good."

Trudy reached out to feel her forehead. "How do you feel?"

"I don't know. Tired mostly."

"Well," Trudy withdrew her hand, "I want you to sleep late tomorrow."

"What about the hospital?"

"You can go in the afternoon."

Meg nodded, too tired to argue. She still wasn't hungry, but picked up her spoon to try the soup.

Trudy sat down on the edge of the bed. "Is there anything you want to talk about?"

"No. Thanks."

"What happened with your friend today?"

Meg scowled. "Nothing."

Trudy nodded, but her eyes looked worried.

They sat quietly, Meg moving the spoon around the bowl of soup without eating any.

"This is what you always worried about," Trudy said.

Meg nodded. Even before her mother had run for President and was just a Senator, Meg worried about security. It was worse when she was a candidate, and the very worst was being in the White House. Not wanting to think about it, she looked up, noticing, for the first time, that Trudy was smaller than she was. Kind of weird. When she was little, she had spent a lot of time on Trudy's lap, playing with her pearls or her crocheting, probably being quite annoying. Lots of times, she would try on her glasses, draping the chain around her neck.

"Are you sure you don't want to talk about it?" Trudy asked.

"Yeah," Meg said. "Very."

She spent the next two days at the hospital, either sitting in her mother's room or waiting to sit in her mother's room. When she was at the White House, she stayed in bed, sometimes reading, but mostly lying down with the lights out, trying to sleep. Being alone was easier than anything else and she left strict instructions with the switchboard not to take calls from anyone other than her parents or Preston. One good thing about the White House—probably the only good thing—was that if you wanted to be alone, it was easy to arrange. No one could get in, or call, without her giving permission. And, right now, she wanted to be alone. Monday, when she would have to go back to school, was more than soon enough to have to deal with people. Even Josh. Especially Josh. She wasn't sure if she was mad at him for not knowing what to do, or mad at herself for being mad at him—but, she was definitely mad. It was easier to avoid him. To avoid everything.

Sunday night, her father came home for the first time, shaky and exhausted. As Meg passed the Presidential Bedroom on her way to the kitchen for some orange juice, he stopped her.

"Could we talk for a minute?" he asked, an untucked Oxford shirt and gray flannel slacks all that remained of the three-piece suit he had had on all day.

In the room, he indicated the couch and she sat down. Something in his expression suggested that it was bad news and she swallowed in advance.

"I'm going to ask you to do something that you won't like," he said, "and I'm also going to ask you to please not argue."

Meg nodded, uneasy.

"I'd like you to drop off the tennis team."

She blinked. "What? There's only two weeks left."

"I know, and I'm sorry, but I don't want you exposing yourself that way. The Secret Service agrees with me."

Meg stared at him. "How am I exposing myself?"

"With—" He hesitated and she saw a muscle near his jaw move. "Everything that's happened, I don't want any of you in situations where you're unnecessarily vulnerable. Tennis courts are practically impossible to protect, Meg, you know that."

"Yeah, but—" He doesn't want me arguing, I shouldn't argue. "I won't get my letter or anything."

"I said I was sorry, Meg."

I'm being a jerk. It's only two weeks. If he really

84

wants me to quit, I should just do it. Even if tennis is the most—"I'm captain, Dad," she said quietly. "How can I quit?"

"They won't survive without you?"

She shook her head. "It's not that. It's just—" Just what? Will you shut up already? But something about having to quit made her feel panicky, made everything seem more real. "Dad, if you want, I'll practice on the courts here. All it is is three stupid matches and the tournament. Nothing's going to happen."

His expression changed so swiftly to fury that she flinched. "Nothing's going to happen?" he asked, his face flushing. "Where the hell have you been for the last week? We're living in a country full of crazies, can't you get that through your head? We get a stack of threatening letters every day, and you're—Jesus, Meg! You think I like this? You think I like knowing that there's nothing I can do to protect any of you? How do you think that makes me feel?"

Meg hunched into her shirt, feeling too guilty to say anything.

"You think I like having to pen all of you up in this place," he gestured around the room and she could see his arms shaking, "because maybe, *maybe* it's safe? Anyone in the country who wants to hurt you can, and there's nothing I can do about it! I was standing two feet from your mother and I still couldn't—I—" He spun away, gripping the footboard of the bed, shaking visibly. "Please leave," he said, his voice thick and almost unfamiliar.

"Dad, I'm sorry, I didn't—"

"Please get out!"

Scared and guilty, she hurried out to the hall, hearing the door close hard behind her. She leaned against a table, trembling herself.

"Meg?" Steven asked, just coming down the hall.

She jerked up. "What? What do you want?"

"You okay?"

No! "Yeah," she said and ran down the hall to her room, slamming the door. She fell back against it, closing

85

her eyes and trying to calm down. Bruce Sampson probably didn't even know how many people he had hurt with his stupid bullets. Steven was right to hate him. She hated him too. More than anything.

CHAPTER ELEVEN

She stayed in her room for the rest of the night, crunched up in bed, reading *Sense and Sensibility* and holding her cat. Sense and sensibility. Yeah, sure. She threw the book across the room and just held Vanessa.

Would someone really hurt her while she was playing tennis? If it was insane to hurt the President, it was even more insane to go after the President's children. How could anyone be that sick?

Her stomach hurt and she held on to it instead of Vanessa, thinking about the afternoons she and Steven and Neal would spend in the Treaty Room, answering the screened letters. Meg tried to get through at least two hundred a week, writing quick scrawling notes on White House stationery. Some letters were funny, some were sad or lonely, some criticized the way she talked or dressed or led her life. A lot of them asked her to give her mother such and such advice. She didn't want to think about the ones she and her brothers never saw.

But now, everything seemed scary, and she had trouble sleeping, dreaming about people with guns firing at her family, people dressed as nurses and orderlies creeping into her mother's room to hurt her—terrible dreams. She would wake up, out of breath, usually crying, and have to turn the light on, holding Vanessa until the fear subsided enough for her to try sleeping again.

And she wasn't the only one who was scared. Her family was, naturally; when she was being taken to the hospital from the car or vice versa, if someone slammed a car door or beeped a horn, she would see her agents flinch.

Everyone seemed to flinch lately, waiting for something to happen, for someone to do something. She closed her eyes, willing her stomach to stop hurting.

There was a knock on the door and she jumped.

"May I come in?" her father asked.

"Uh, yeah. I mean, sure."

He opened the door, and while his expression was composed, he seemed a little shaky and very sad. "I'm sorry I lost control," he said.

"It's okay." Meg blushed, feeling as if she were giving absolution. "I mean, it's probably good for you."

"In any case, I'm sorry."

"I'm sorry I argued."

"Well, I didn't expect you to be thrilled about the idea." He put his hands into his pockets, looking old and hunched. "I wouldn't do it if I didn't feel that it was necessary."

"H-have they gotten any more threats?" Meg asked. "Like last summer?"

"No. Your mother and I just want to take as many precautions as we can." He sighed. "I really am sorry. The last thing I want to do is hurt my children."

"You're not hurting us."

"I'm not helping very much either."

It was awkwardly silent.

"Well." Her father sighed. "Good night. Sleep well."

"Um, yeah," Meg said. "You too."

Her stomach hurt the next morning, so she skipped breakfast, staying in her room to fold and refold her tennis uniform, smoothing out all of the wrinkles, hoping that she was going to be able to get through the day. Right now, she felt like going inside her closet, closing the door, and never coming out.

But it was getting late, and she went down to the dining room to say good-bye. Her mother's chair was very empty—instead of sitting there, Trudy had been sitting in an extra chair on Meg's side of the table.

"If you hurry," Trudy said, "you have time for some cereal and juice."

Meg shook her head. "No, thanks. I'm not all that hungry."

"At least have some juice."

Meg gulped part of a glass of orange juice, her stomach rebelling all the way. "See you guys later." She glanced at her father. "Tell Mom I said hi and hope she's feeling better and everything."

He nodded, his eyes almost as tired as they had been the night before. "Have a nice day," he said, either from force of habit, or to make it seem like a normal morning.

"Yeah, you too."

"Meggie, wait!" Steven called after her. "Later," he said to the others, his typical tough-kid good-bye.

Meg waited in the Center Hall, reflecting briefly and bitterly on the fact that it was probably the first school day all year that she hadn't had to bring her tennis racket. For once, everything would fit in her locker. Big deal.

"Um, look," Steven said, his eyes on his sneakers, ankle-high basketball Nikes. "I'm sorry."

"About what?"

"Tennis. You must feel pretty bad."

Yeah. "It doesn't matter," she said. "The season's almost over anyway. What's the deal on basketball?"

Steven kicked the carpet. "It might be okay because it's indoors and they can just like, put on extra guards."

"Oh," Meg said. Don't sound jealous. No point in making him feel lousy too. "Well, that's good. I mean, I'm glad."

"Are you, um," he didn't look up, "mad at me?"

Insanely jealous is more like it. "No."

"It's not my fault."

"I know. Don't worry about it."

"Well, are you sure? I mean," he blinked several times, "if you want, I'll quit too so you'll like, have company."

What a nice guy. "No, don't be dumb." She managed a grin. "The season's almost over anyway. It doesn't matter."

"You sure?"

"Yes."

"You don't hate me?"

Instead of answering, she punched him in the ribs and he grinned. "Guess you don't," he said.

"Right," she said. "Come on, we're late."

There were reporters outside and cameras everywhere, many more than usual, and for a second, Meg didn't think she was going to be able to go out there. But she could tell that Steven was scared too, and walking him over to his car before going to hers gave her time to find enough courage to get back to *her* car and inside. Security was extra tight and she rode silently with her regular day agents, another car with two more agents following them.

On the ride, she thought about her mother. If she was up yet, what she was doing. If they were letting her eat regular food. If she hurt as much as she had yesterday. If the agents driving her father to the hospital would be able to protect him. If—they were at the school now, and she saw bunches of reporters outside, almost as many as had been there on her first day of school. Seeing the car, they swarmed over in her direction, still more agents blocking them back. Meg gripped her knapsack with both hands, afraid to get out of the car.

"You okay?" one of her agents asked.

She didn't answer, staring at the crowd, the school looking completely unfamiliar. The agents from the car behind them opened her door and hesitantly, she climbed out. The cameras were rolling, reporters were shouting and shoving microphones at her, and she froze, afraid to move.

"How do you feel about—"

"—afraid for your mother's safety?"

"—true that you're no longer allowed to play on the—"

"Come on," Wayne, one of her agents, said in her ear, "let's get inside."

She still hung back against the car, and then agents had each of her arms, propelling her almost painfully through the crowd and inside, other agents keeping the press out of the building.

The hall was also crowded, with students and a few teachers, all of whom were staring at her. There was a phone alcove off the lobby and she walked swiftly over, sitting down and closing the door to have some privacy, trying to calm down. She held the phone so it would look like she was making a call, eyes tightly shut.

Don't cry, she ordered herself. You can't cry—everyone will see. She gripped the phone, taking slow deep breaths. Her agents were outside, looking very concerned, and it looked as if even more people had crowded into the hall to see what was going on. She took two more deep breaths, then stood up, opening the door.

"Are you all right?" Gary, her other agent, asked quietly.

She nodded, not looking up in case her eyes were red. "I have to go see Mrs. Ferris."

"We can have someone take care of that for you."

She shook her head, walking down the hall, people moving out of her way. No one said anything to her and she was half-relieved, half-hurt, focusing on the floor.

Her coach, who was also a history teacher, was sitting behind the desk in her tenth grade homeroom. Meg knocked on the door and Mrs. Ferris, seeing her, came out to the hall.

"It's good to have you back," she said. "How is everything?"

"Fine, thank you." Meg pulled the uniform out of her knapsack, resisting the urge to touch the red-lettered CAPTAIN one last time. "Uh, I'm really sorry, but I'm kind of not allowed to play anymore."

Her coach nodded. "Your father's press secretary spoke to me."

"Yeah, well," Meg swallowed, tears suddenly hot in her eyes. "I guess—"

Mrs. Ferris touched her arm. "I'm sorry. Is there anything I can do?"

"I don't think so, but thank you." Meg gave her the uniform and hurried down the hall before she started crying.

She managed to make it to her locker and homeroom without breaking down, but could tell from the trembling tension of her arms and legs that it was going to be a very difficult day. As she walked into the room, people stopped whatever they were doing, awkward and uneasy. She crossed to her desk, sitting with her shoulders hunched, hating being the focus of attention. She saw Alison coming over and abruptly turned her back, making it obvious that she didn't want to talk to anyone. She heard Alison hesitate, then move away.

Homeroom was very quiet, no one bothering her. When the bell rang, she let everyone else leave first, pretending to fumble through her knapsack. Walking to the door, she saw Josh in the hall, tense against a locker. He approached tentatively, both hands in his pockets.

Don't hug me, she thought. She'd fall apart if he hugged her right now.

Everyone in the hall was staring at her, as if she had lost a limb or been horribly burned or something, and no one knew how to treat her anymore.

"Uh, hi," he said.

"I want to be alone," she said stiffly.

"Oh." He stopped. "Well, I just—"

"Try listening to me, how about?"

"I'm sorry."

"What, is sorry your new word?"

He stepped back uneasily. "No, I—I mean—"

"Well, quit saying it, okay?" she asked, his nervousness annoying her even more. He was supposed to be her closest friend, for Christ's sakes. What was he doing being afraid of her?

"Meg—" He hesitated. "Is it okay if I walk with you?"

"You have to ask permission?"

"No. I just—I don't know what you want me to do."

She released an irritated breath. "Right now, that might not be such a great question, Josh."

"I'm sorry. I mean—" His expression was very unhappy. "I just don't want to upset you."

"Too bad, because you're doing a hell of a job." She moved past him and down the hall, knowing that he wouldn't come after her. None of this was his fault—why did she keep yelling at him? She couldn't tell if she felt like falling down and crying, or turning around and hitting someone.

People were staring at her and she gave the entire hall a mean look, afraid that if anyone came near her, she might do something irrational. Like she had just done.

Her whole French class stopped talking when she came in and she had to gulp, suddenly very nauseated. There was an empty seat in the back and she took it, praying that no one would come over to her. Luckily, either people seemed to sense it, or word had gotten around that she wanted to be left alone.

Once class started, her teacher's voice sounded like the robot-teacher in the Charlie Brown cartoons, and she looked at her desk, concentrating on not throwing up. If he called on her, she would probably pass out.

Neal was on his way to school now—were his agents taking care of him? He was so small. It was awful to think of a crowd of agents surrounding an eight-year-old. Was he as scared as she had been? As she still was?

When the bell rang, her stomach jumped as much as she did.

"Mademoiselle Powers?" her teacher asked.

Great. She was going to throw up all over Mr. Thénardier. She walked up to the front of the room, gripping her knapsack.

"Ah, Mademoiselle Powers," he said. "I wanted to—"

"Could I talk to you tomorrow, sir?" she asked. "I'm not feeling very well."

"Of course," he said. "Would you like me to take you down to the clinic?"

"No, thank you." She returned to her desk, taking deep breaths. She didn't want to throw up. If she did, she would never live it down. No one ever forgot people who threw up at school. She had a brief memory flash of Anne-Marie Hammersmith throwing up all over the place in the third grade. During geography. The last she'd heard, Anne-Marie lost the election for Junior Prom Queen. She was incredibly beautiful, so it was probably because of people who remembered her throwing up. No one ever forgot.

Only now she had to go to physics. The last time she had gone to physics . . . Wishing for something, *anything*, to get her out of class—how would that make her mother feel if she knew? *She* felt like King Midas.

She veered over to the nearest water fountain, pretending to take a drink, but really hanging on for support. But before her agents could talk to her, she started walking again, her legs weak. The science lab didn't have any windows—like the waiting room at the hospital, when they were waiting to find out—she pulled her sweater sleeve across her face, ordering herself not to be dizzy. She found an empty seat near the door and opened her book, the page blurring in front of her eyes.

As her teacher began his lecture, she hung on to her book, the corners digging into her hands. She should be taking notes, but she was afraid to move and get a pen, afraid the motion would make her feel worse. Her teacher's voice was as blurred as the pages had been and seemed unnaturally loud.

"Hey," someone next to her whispered. "You okay?"

She nodded, sucking in a deep, nausea-controlling breath. It didn't work and she shoved away from her desk, running out of the room. She ran down the hall to the nearest girls' lav and inside, her agents right behind her. There were three girls standing around with cigarettes who stared, dropped them into a sink, and hurried out.

"Meg," one of her agents said, "are you—"

"Leave me alone!" She leaned against the wall, resting her head on her arms, fists tight.

"We just have to make sure you're all right," he said, but she could also hear them checking the room to make sure that there was no one else in there, no potential threat. Oh yeah, they were *great* at their jobs.

"Okay," Wayne said, "we'll—"

"Jesus Christ!" She whirled around, her face flushing with a sudden hot fury. "Can't I even throw up in private?"

They nodded, both edging towards the door.

"You follow me everywhere," Meg said, her voice shaking, "make my stupid life miserable, and then, *then,* when we goddamn need you, no one's around! Mom probably would have been better off without you! All you do is make things worse! *Tempt* people to hurt us!"

"Meg," Wayne said quietly, "calm—"

"Don't tell me what to do! You're not my parents—you're not anybody! You're just stupid jerks who can't even do their jobs!"

"Meg," he put a gentle hand on her shoulder, "just—"

She jerked away. *"Touch* me, and I'm getting new agents! I don't have to put up with that!"

"Okay." He moved to the door. "We'll be right outside."

"Of course," she nodded. "A bunch of professional voyeurs. Professional *cowards."*

Neither man said anything.

"What would you do if someone was in here, anyway? Let them shoot me a couple of times and *then,* react?"

Still neither spoke.

"Oh, I forgot," she said. "I'm the President's daughter. God forbid any of you talk to me." She shook her head. "I should have figured. If you're scared to *talk* to us, naturally you're going to be scared to protect us. Jerks." She pushed

95

past them and out to the hall, every muscle trembling, fists clenched to keep from bursting into reaction tears. She stopped. ''By the way,'' she said. ''Thanks for getting me kicked off tennis.''

CHAPTER TWELVE

She went straight to the car, not even stopping by the office to let them know that she was leaving. She slouched in the backseat, not speaking to any of her agents, and they drove her home in silence. At least the stupid reporters were gone.

At the White House, she left the car without her usual thank-you, going directly upstairs to her room and putting on her nightgown. Trudy came in with ginger ale and fussed over her for a while—tucking her in, fluffing her pillows, adjusting the window shades. She assured Trudy that she was fine and just needed to sleep, and everyone left her alone.

She was still too upset to sleep, so she picked up the phone and called the chief usher. It was Monday, and *Newsweek* and *Time* and the other weeklies would be out. He was reluctant to send them up to her—her parents had probably asked that the magazines be kept away from the three of them—but she insisted and a butler brought up several.

Her mother was on all of the covers except for one, which had a picture of the Presidential Seal with a silhouette of a gun in front of it. Two of the covers were closeups of her mother's expression as the bullets hit: surprised pain. Eyebrows up and startled, mouth tightening in a wince. The fourth cover was a picture of her seconds before; smiling, arm lifting in a wave, framed by blue and gray suited agents.

She dropped the magazines in her lap, afraid to look inside. The prevalent message on the covers was *"Again?"* And again and again and again.

She opened the first magazine and found the usual five

or six stories associated with assassination attempts: the editorial lament; the minute-by-minute account; the biography and personal profile of the gunman, along with a rehash of other assassins from Lee Harvey Oswald on; the requisite article about the challenge faced by security agents; the article describing every detail of the doctors' work. All accompanied by pictures in living color. Terrific. Some enterprising person was always there taking pictures of leaders crumpling in agony. You had to wonder about the kind of people who could do that.

There were lots of pictures of the assassin. He was smirking in most of them, and quoted saying things like, "Too bad I missed" and "Guess that showed *her*." It wasn't like there was any doubt that he was insane. Insanity was no excuse.

There was only one post-shooting picture of her mother, one her press secretary, Linda, had released of a staff meeting in her hospital room. There weren't any pictures of her walking around, "on the road to recovery," since she still couldn't *sit up* for extended periods of time.

There were pictures of Vice-President Kruger, of important staff and cabinet members, all working to keep the United States government going. Pictures of her father, very pale, appearing not to have slept in days. There was even a picture of her, going into the hospital with Neal and Steven the morning after it happened. She had one hand in Neal's, the other on Steven's shoulder, and the three of them looked very grim. The President's children demonstrating public composure.

The coverage in the magazines was pretty much the same. Some of the pictures were duplicates, some were just different angles. She was in all four: with Steven and Neal, the same picture, in two; then, in the third, she was alone, rushing into the hospital right after it happened, her eyes dark and huge. Again, composed terror. The one in the fourth magazine was the worst because she couldn't remember its being taken except that she was wearing her gray Levi's, so it must have been Saturday. She was sitting alone on a bench in a hospital corridor, with her elbows on her knees, her face in her hands. The First Daughter, in a moment of private grief, the caption said. And it *was* private. It didn't seem right that they could publish that in a national magazine. She looked small and scared and as if she were trying as hard as she could to hold herself together. The kind of picture *Life* would print in its Year-in-Review issue. Not very fair.

The articles talked about her mother's courage, the physically fragile woman and her incredible inner strength. About her gallantry, her unquenchable sense of humor. About an Administration so well managed that "the wheels of government continued turning without a hitch." About Vice-President Kruger's superb clutch leadership and reactions to the incident from world leaders, all of whom were appalled—her mother was very well-liked.

And the articles talked about the family. "Public composure" was the big phrase. Public composure and private agony. Loving family shattered by gunfire. And her mother had jumped a good ten points in the polls. What a way to do it.

She pushed the magazines onto the floor, sick of reading about it. The thing the magazines ignored was that all of them were real people. The stories were glib, play-by-play analyses without any emotion. Stories that were, after all, out to sell magazines. Maybe even to entertain.

"That the best you can do for reading material?" Preston asked from the door.

"They're pretty bad," she said.

"I know, kid. That's why the three of you weren't supposed to see them." He was wearing dark brown flannel pants with a brown, tan and white Argyle V-neck, a white shirt and skinny brown tie underneath. His loafers were so shiny that it looked as if people carried him around all the time so his feet wouldn't touch the floor. "How you feeling?" he asked.

She shrugged.

"Too shiny?"

She looked up. "What?"

"My shoes."

"Oh. Well, yeah," she nodded. "They look too new."

"They *are* new."

"Oh."

He smiled. "I really wonder what goes on in your head, kid."

She shrugged.

"What's going on in it right now?"

"Nothing much."

"You've been reading those," he indicated the magazines, "and nothing's going on in your head?"

"Not really," she said stiffly.

"Well, I envy you, kid. I think I'd be going crazy."

She shrugged.

"Not that it's not upsetting anyway. Your family is very important to me." He looked right at her and she nodded self-consciously. "How do you feel?" he asked, his voice gentle.

She sighed and shook her head. How many people were going to ask her that?

"Public composure," he said.

"Yeah."

"Have you had lunch?"

"I'm not hungry."

"Well, *I* am," he said. "And I missed breakfast too."

"Is the mess still open?" she asked uncertainly. Most White House people ate in a special dining room downstairs. "Or you could have someone in the kitchen make you something."

"I thought we could cook."

"What do you mean, *we?*"

"Throw on some clothes," he said. "I'll go tell Carl we're taking over."

"We are?"

"Yeah. Hurry it up." He closed the door as he left and, not sure what else to do, Meg got out of bed, changing into sweat pants, a blue flannel shirt, and her Topsiders. She always wore her Topsiders around the house because slippers looked stupid. Once, someone had given her a pair of slippers that looked like pink fuzzy rabbits and she had had to wear them to be polite, in spite of the fact that she felt like an idiot. Slippers were not cool.

Preston was alone in the kitchen, wearing a brown apron. It figured that even his apron would be color-co-ordinated.

"Where is everyone?" she asked.

"I gave them a break." He handed her a glass of dark liquid. "Want a Tab?"

"Well, yeah. I guess." She sipped some, watching him rummage through the refrigerator. Preston wasn't a person she thought of as an industrious little cook.

"What are you in the mood for, kid?" he asked.

"Do you cook?"

"What do you think—I go home, open cans of ravioli, and eat them cold?"

She frowned. "I never really thought about it."

"Well, think about it," he said, turning the heat on underneath the kettle on the stove for coffee.

"What's your apartment like?"

He grinned. "Immaculate. What do you want to make?"

"Sandwiches?"

"Sounds pretty boring, don't you think?"

"I guess." She sat at the table. "Um, do you have a better idea?"

"I was thinking along the lines of a glutinous pasta concoction."

"Okay," Meg said, suddenly feeling hungry.

"Great." He opened the refrigerator. "Your job is to create something absolutely wonderful for dessert."

"Dessert?"

"You have no idea how hungry I am, kid." He opened the cupboard where the baking supplies were kept. "Here. Use your imagination."

At first, the whole thing seemed kind of dumb, but Preston's enthusiasm was contagious and the cooking started being fun. He was frying mushrooms and onions and peppers, which he assured her were an integral part of his pasta plan. End quote. She was whipping cream. When he asked her why, she said that it was an integral part of her dessert plan, which was a lie. Actually, she had no plan whatsoever, but whipping cream might give her enough time to think of one. Not that she wouldn't be happy slopping the cream onto graham crackers and eating them without further adornment. But Preston probably had a more discerning palate. *Most* people probably did.

They ate in the West Sitting Hall. Preston had combined his sautéed vegetables with noodles and lots of cheese and butter and it was one of the better pasta concoctions she had ever eaten. He had also made a salad: spinach, romaine and Boston lettuce, cucumber slivers, purple onions, carrots. She drank Tab and he had coffee and they didn't talk about anything difficult: just basketball and skiing and their favorite paintings in the White House and Great Meals They Had Known. She felt better than she had in days.

"Well, kid." He sat back. "Let's see this dessert of yours."

"Okay, but you have to wait here." She carried their plates to the kitchen. "I'll just be a minute."

She scraped and rinsed the plates, trying to think. Maybe she would have to go with graham crackers. She took down two nice hefty bowls and broke graham crackers into them. The freezer had chocolate and chocolate-chip ice cream and she filled the bowls with alternating spoonfuls of the two flavors. Then, she sprinkled chocolate chips on top, making chocolate sauce with Nestle's Quik and hot water, pouring it over the chips. She added more than generous spoonfuls of whipped cream. But she needed one final—*elle ne savait quoi*—there were some Oreos and she crushed a few, covering the whipped cream with the pieces. She stuck a spoon in each and carried them out to the table.

Preston grinned. "Way to go, kid."

"It's an old family recipe."

"I can tell."

They talked about Baskin-Robbins ice cream, Woody Allen movies, and the best Robert Parker mysteries they had ever read, Meg feeling so relaxed that she finished her entire dish of ice cream.

"What a little piglet," Preston observed.

She grunted cooperatively. "How come you're not over at the hospital or anything?"

"Because I wanted to have lunch with you."

"To cheer the little kid up?"

He shrugged. "Why not?"

"Hunh." She played with the sauce and melted ice cream left in her dish.

"Steven's pretty upset with his agents."

Meg looked up sharply. Was that meant for her? "Oh," she said. "Did they do something?"

"I guess he's blaming them for your mother being shot."

Meg flinched at the word "shot." How could he come right out and say it?

"Meg?"

"Sounds pretty immature," she said.

He shrugged. "People do pretty funny things when they're upset."

Meg let out her breath, annoyed. Preston didn't usually play games. "What, did my agents fink on me or something?"

"They didn't 'fink.' They're worried about you, Meg."

"They should be, if they have that much trouble protecting people."

"Is that really fair?" he asked.

"What difference does it make?"

"I don't know." He drank some coffee. "Bert Travis's family is probably feeling pretty lousy about the whole thing."

"He's not even on crutches," Meg said, irritated.

Preston shrugged. "He could have been killed."

"Yeah, well, so could—" She stopped. "Forget it, I don't want to talk about it."

"You know," he said, "Sometimes things like this make families even closer."

"What do you do in your free time—read Hallmark cards?"

He shrugged. "Everyone needs a hobby."

Meg frowned, not amused.

"It's just something to think about," he said. "Want another Tab?"

"No."

"Feel like hitting a few?" He made a tennis swing with his arm.

"Why? I'm not allowed to play anymore."

"You might feel better if you got some exercise."

"Oh," she nodded, "so now I'm fat?"

"No. Just thought it might make you feel better." He reached across the table to pat her shoulder, then collected the dishes, carrying them out to the kitchen.

"Are you mad?" Meg asked when he returned.

"Should I be?"

"Well," she didn't look at him, "I guess I was pretty rude."

"So you were rude," he said, shrugging. "Doesn't bother me."

"Yeah, but—"

"Just be selective," he said. "You want to be rude, come find me."

Meg frowned uncertainly. "I don't get it."

"You don't want to take things out on the wrong people, that's all."

"What, you mean my agents?"

"Your agents," he agreed. "Your friends. Anyone who isn't directly involved."

Meg folded her arms. Was he bugging her about Josh now? Nothing like having a private life.

"Can't keep these things inside, kid," he said. "You do, and they come out at all the wrong times, you know?"

Meg didn't say anything.

"You have to find someone to talk to. It doesn't have

to be me, but—'' He paused. ''If you don't talk about it, you'll drive yourself crazy.''

Meg looked at her hands.

''Well,'' he said. ''I guess I've annoyed you enough.''

She nodded.

''Then maybe I'll head back over,'' he said. ''Unless you feel like hitting a few, or checking out MTV or something.''

She shook her head.

''Okay. Whatever.'' He stood up. ''You know where to find me.''

She nodded.

''Good.'' He bent to kiss the top of her head. ''Thanks for letting me have lunch with you.''

''*Letting* you?''

He looked sad. ''You didn't have a nice time?''

She had to grin. ''It was swell.''

When he was gone, she sat at the table for a long time, thinking. He was right—she had to talk to *someone*. But, this wasn't exactly a great time to talk to Josh. And if she couldn't talk to Josh, who—she glanced over at the clock on the side table. Going on to four. That meant school had been out for—she crossed over to the telephone, picking it up and dialing.

Beth answered.

''Um, hi,'' Meg said.

''Oh, hi,'' Beth said. ''What's up?''

''Nothing. I mean, things are—I don't know. Pretty bad.'' She swallowed. ''I was wondering, um—do you think you can maybe still come here?''

''Sure,'' Beth said. ''When?''

CHAPTER THIRTEEN

Beth took an evening shuttle down, the White House sending a car out to the airport to pick her up. Meg was just as happy to stay at the White House and avoid her agents. She waited downstairs in the Diplomatic Reception Room, slouching on a yellow sofa. Since she wasn't in the family quarters, her agents *were* around, but at least they weren't making themselves obvious.

"The car is arriving, Miss Powers," a Marine guard told her from the door.

"Thanks." She went out through the South Entrance to wait.

One of the inevitable black cars pulled up and Beth got out before they could open the door for her.

"Hi," she said, grinning.

Meg had to grin back, especially at her rust felt hat, a small feather in the band. "Nice hat."

"Fall," Beth said and glanced around. "I was kind of expecting photographers."

"Disappointed?"

"Yeah, actually." She picked up her overnight bag and a B. Dalton bag and they looked at each other. "Never done much hugging, have we?"

"Not really," Meg said.

"Well. No point in starting now."

"Not really."

"Yeah." Beth's grin came back. "Then again, what the hell?" She gave Meg a quick hug, then continued past her into the house.

"You're really weird," Meg said, following her.

"But, *oh* so charming," Beth said.

"Yeah, right."

Beth stopped on the red carpet outside the Diplomatic Reception Room, looking up and down the Ground Floor Corridor, at the Presidential Seal, at the portraits of First Ladies. "This place could grow on me."

"Oh, yeah," Meg said. "It's terrific."

Beth pointed at the paintings of Jacqueline Kennedy and Eleanor Roosevelt. "Those don't impress you?"

"No."

"That's what I like about you," Beth said, draping her arm over Meg's shoulders. "You're so much fun to be with." She dropped her arm. "Your brothers here?"

"Yeah, upstairs. Dad's still at the hospital."

"How's your mother?"

Meg shook her head, crossing the hall to the main staircase.

They found Steven and Neal up in the solarium with Trudy, watching a tape of *The Last Starfighter*.

"Hi, Mrs. Donovan," Beth said cheerfully. "Hi, guys." She hefted the bookstore bag. "Better stop the tape—it's present time."

"Records?" Meg guessed.

Beth laughed. "Can't pull the wool over *your* eyes, can I?"

"How was your flight, Beth?" Trudy asked, as Steven put the VCR on pause.

"Well, exhausting," Beth said, "but—"

"The whole hour and a half," Meg interrupted.

Beth laughed. "Yeah. But, my God, I remember my last flight to Zimbabwe—"

Trudy also laughed, standing up. "I have some brownies and cocoa downstairs waiting for all of you."

"Not," Beth said, "double chocolate with butterscotch chips."

Trudy nodded, smiling.

"Invite me more often," Beth said to Meg.

"No, don't worry," Trudy said as Meg moved to help her. "You four just wait up here."

Beth sat down on the couch next to Steven and Neal. "How are you guys?"

They both shrugged.

"What do you think of the hat, Steven?" she asked.

He shrugged again. "Pretty queer."

"I agree." Beth put it on Neal's head, and Neal giggled. "Now, then." She reached into her bag, pulling out a gift-wrapped present with a red ribbon. "This one's for your mother and," she reached back in, coming out with a blue-ribboned hardcover, *"this* one's for your father."

Meg leaned over to see the title. *A Woodsman's Journal.* "Good choice."

"Well, thank you, Meghan." Beth reached back into the bag.

"How come Mom's is wrapped and Dad's isn't?" Neal asked.

"Because your mother always used to say, 'Pretty wrapping makes the experience complete,' and your father would say, 'Oh, for God's sakes.' "

Meg studied her, impressed. "You have a hell of a memory."

"It's a curse," Beth said sadly.

"So, where's my present?" Meg asked.

"Well, okay, so I brought *most* of you presents." Beth pulled out a Hardy Boys book—number eighteen, *The Twisted Claw.* "My personal favorite," she said, and handed it to Neal.

"Hey, wow, thanks!" Neal said, sitting back to check it out.

"And this," Beth took out *The Sandy Koufax Story* and gave it to Steven, "is for you. An educational gift," she remarked to Meg. "Both inspirational and precautionary."

"I don't suppose you have anything in that bag for me," Meg said, being Dorothy in *The Wizard of Oz.*

"Pay no attention to that man behind the curtain," Beth said and handed her a thick paperback.

Meg studied the cover—splashy and trashy, lots of embracing—then turned the book over, feeling the spine. "The binding's broken."

"Well, sure," Beth said. "I had to read it and make sure there was plenty of sex." She grinned. "There is."

Trudy came up with cocoa and brownies, and they watched the rest of *The Last Starfighter*, Beth lightening the atmosphere considerably. After saying hello to Meg's father, they ended up in Meg's room, Meg slouched on the bed and Beth studying her shelf of records.

"Your father looks even worse than you do," she remarked.

"Yeah," Meg agreed. "He's not sleeping much."

Beth nodded, then straightened up. "You need more Motown."

"They have just about every damn record in the world upstairs."

"Well, we'll just have to make do," Beth said, her voice long-suffering. She pulled a record out. "Can you do without Joan Jett?"

"I love Joan Jett," Meg said automatically.

"I know you do." Beth held up *Ghost in the Machine*, by the Police. "Let's compromise." She put the record on, then bent over her overnight bag, pulling out a pack of Newports. She held them up. "Want to get over on the Establishment?"

Meg grinned. "Wow, you are just too cool."

"Wait, it gets better." Beth opened the door. "Come on."

"Come on *where?*"

"Just come on."

Meg followed her out to the hall, Beth walking as cautiously as a cat burglar.

"Be careful," Beth stage-whispered. "We don't want to be seen."

"Oh, well, lucky we're in the White House," Meg said. "No one's *ever* around."

"Shh," Beth hissed, and slunk down the Center Hall a few feet.

"You're what," Meg said, "a senior now?"

"Shh, you want to blow our cover?" Beth flattened

against the doorway leading to the West Sitting Hall. "You think it's clear?"

"If Carl is off-duty."

"We'll have to chance it," Beth said grimly, and crept down to the kitchen.

Meg, starting to get amused, followed her.

"What do you think?" Beth asked, crouching in the hallway leading to the kitchen. "Do we go for it?"

"Well, I don't know," Meg said. "What's the primary goal?"

"I call it—Operation Heineken."

Meg laughed.

"Look," Beth said, "if you're scared, just say so. No one will ever have to know."

"No fear here," Meg said.

"Good." Beth took a deep, shuddering breath. "This is a very emotional moment."

"See you on the other side," Meg said.

Beth nodded, then released the breath, darting into the kitchen. She ran her hands across the front of the refrigerator, as though testing for alarms, then opened the door a centimeter at a time. Her arm snaked inside, pulling out one bottle of beer, then another. "Try to find an opener," she whispered.

Meg nodded, easing the silverware drawer open and extricating one.

"All right." Beth wiped her sleeve across her face. "Now, look. Just be cool. Anyone stops us, and you just keep going, you hear me? *Just keep going.*"

Meg laughed.

"Damn it, this is no time for levity!"

"Sorry," Meg said.

Beth nodded impatiently. "Let's just get out of here." She stuck her head out into the hall, looking both ways. She nodded at Meg, motioning for her to follow. They were almost to the Center Hall when Beth stopped dead, Meg, naturally, crashing into her.

"What is it?" Meg asked, almost uneasy in spite of herself.

"I *tripped* the *sensors*," Beth said, her voice horrified. "What do we do?"

"Run like crazy!" Beth ran down the hall to Meg's room, closing the door after Meg was inside and leaning against it, out of breath. Then, she looked up, grinning. "Was that fun?"

"Lots," Meg said.

"Good." Beth handed her the beers. "Open these, and *I'll* put on our favorite song." She took out a Commodores album, setting it to "Brick House."

"Our favorite fantasy, more likely," Meg said.

"For *you*, maybe," Beth said, dancing slightly as she lit her cigarette.

Meg watched her. "Boy, do you have rhythm."

Beth nodded, dancing. *"Everyone* says so."

"Keep it up, and you'll be on 'Solid Gold' in no time."

Beth nodded. "It's what I live for." She stopped, seeing that Meg was sitting in one of the chairs by the fireplace. "What, you're not having fun?"

"Lots," Meg said. "Really."

"Well, we'll have to remedy *that*." Beth danced over to the record shelf, checking the titles. "Oh no, I don't believe how queer you are. You actually *bought* the sound track for *Ghostbusters?*"

"Bet you did too."

"Damn straight," Beth said, pulling the album out. She put the title track on, dancing to that instead.

"If you want," Meg said, "I have 'Dancing with Myself.' "

Beth stopped. "You're *still* not having fun?"

Meg shrugged.

"Well, it's no good if you're not having fun." Beth looked at her for a minute, then sighed deeply. "Oh, *all right.*"

"What?"

Beth just sighed, crossing to the shelf, pulling a record out and putting it on the stereo. *"Now* are you happy?"

Meg grinned as Joan Jett's "I Love Rock and Roll" blasted out of the stereo. "Yeah," she said. "I am."

* * *

Beth was supposed to fly home late the next afternoon, so Meg had permission to stay home from school. They had stayed up pretty late, watching David Letterman and then strolling down to the kitchen for a second beer, so they both slept until almost eleven.

"Is anyone else here?" Beth asked, wandering into the West Sitting Hall where Meg was drinking orange juice and patting Vanessa.

Meg shook her head. "Just the Cast of Thousands." She and Steven had always called the White House staff the Cast of Thousands. "Are you hungry? They can make us something."

Beth looked uneasy. "You don't feel funny asking?"

"They feel funny if I *don't* ask."

They ended up at the table in the West Sitting Hall, the kitchen serving them a huge breakfast of juice, melon, toast, muffins, doughnuts, eggs, bacon, sausage, and milk.

"I sure would be fat if I lived here," Beth said.

Meg shrugged. "On school days, I mostly just have cereal."

They ate without saying much.

"Pretty tough week," Beth said.

"Yeah," Meg said, more stiffly.

"At least she's getting better."

Meg shrugged.

Beth started to say something else, but helped herself to more bacon instead.

"I don't feel like talking about what happened," Meg said.

Beth helped herself to some eggs too. "Then, we won't."

Meg nodded.

"If you want," Beth said, "we could go listen to 'I Love Rock and Roll.' "

Meg shook her head. "I'm sorry. I'm being a jerk. I'm just kind of tired."

"Then, let's go upstairs and put Mel Gibson movies on."

"That sounds okay," Meg said, her bad mood fading somewhat.

They sat up in the solarium with glasses of orange juice, watching *Gallipoli*.

"You sure have a lot of phone messages in your room," Beth remarked.

"To be honest with you," Meg said, "I haven't even looked at them."

"There are probably a couple from me in there."

"Yeah." Meg shifted her position. "I don't know. I guess I haven't really felt like talking to anyone."

Beth nodded.

"It's easier not to, you know?"

Beth nodded. "What's the deal with Josh?"

Meg scowled into her orange juice glass. "What do you mean?"

"I just kind of figured he'd be around. You haven't even *mentioned* him."

Meg shrugged, tightly gripping her glass.

"You guys have a fight or something?"

"Yeah, I guess. I mean—" Meg let out her breath. "God, I don't know. One minute, he was at the hospital and I was really glad he was there, and the next minute, he was bugging the hell out of me, you know?"

Beth shook her head.

"I don't know." Meg sighed. "It's like, he just stood there and let me yell at him. He didn't do *anything.*"

"I'd be mad too," Beth said.

"No, you don't understand. He was acting like we didn't even know each other or something. Like I was the President's daughter and he was some, I don't know, *peon* or something." She glanced over at Beth's expression. "I'm not explaining it right."

"So, explain it," Beth said, shrugging.

"It's like he didn't know what to do at all. Like, I yelled

at him and he just got all nervous and scared. Then, at school, he was doing the same thing. Looking like he thought I was going to *hit* him or something.''

''Maybe he thought you were going to.''

''Oh, yeah, right,'' Meg said. ''What was he, threatened?''

Beth didn't say anything.

''Yeah, well, he shouldn't do that,'' Meg said defensively. ''I mean, part of it—*most* of it, even—was that I was mad in general, not at him. I mean—'' She shook her head. ''We've been seeing each other for a hell of a long time—I should be able to yell at him, you know?''

''What, because you're close, you should be able to abuse him?''

''Well—yeah,'' Meg said. ''I mean—you know what I mean. I can yell at *you* and *you* don't do anything.''

''It's different,'' Beth said.

''No, it isn't. I mean, *Christ.* For all I know, we're going to—'' She flushed slightly. ''Well, you know.''

''No,'' Beth brought her eyebrows together in pretended confusion, ''I don't.''

''Don't be a jerk.''

''But,'' Beth's eyebrows moved still closer, ''I really don't—''

''*Sleep* together, for Christ's sakes!''

''Oh. That.'' Beth grinned. ''What, you think that's a big deal?''

Meg was about to get mad, but she forced herself to take a slow, deep breath. ''Am I the only one who knows that you talk a lot?''

''Don't spread it around.''

''Yeah, right.'' Meg slouched down, staring at *Gallipoli* without watching it. ''It *is* a big deal,'' she said quietly.

Beth nodded. ''If you think about it, Meg, you're lucky to be in a position to be considering it.''

Meg considered *that.* ''Still the same old losers at our school, hunh?''

''Pretty much. Anyway,'' Beth swung her feet onto the

114

coffee table, "you know me. I've got a thing for older men."

"You don't *know* any older men."

"I know." Beth looked sad. "I guess it's my own private hell."

"You are *such* an asshole."

"I know," Beth said.

They were companionably silent.

"I couldn't say that to anyone in this whole stupid city without them getting all hurt or mad or something—even Josh." Meg sighed. *"Especially* Josh."

Beth nodded.

"It's like, I don't have *friends* anymore."

"Oh, come on," Beth said.

"It's true. I mean, it's not the same."

"Did you expect it to be?"

Meg slouched lower. "I don't know."

"It changed at home too," Beth pointed out. "By the convention, even Sarah was treating you funny."

"Yeah," Meg said, remembering how, as the primary and election season had progressed, people she had known half of her life—like Sarah Weinberger—had been so intimidated that they barely spoke to her anymore. She glanced over. "I was afraid you were going to get weird too."

"I was *already* weird," Beth said.

"You know what I mean."

"My God, Meg, I remember you sitting in first grade, crying."

"My ear practically *ruptured* that day," Meg said defensively.

"Yeah, I know. It's just—" Now it was Beth's turn to shift her position—"If I get weirded out, I think about things like that."

Meg nodded, her hand automatically cupping her ear with the memory. They were supposed to be writing their sentences while their teacher, Mrs. Stokes, worked with a reading group. Meg had sat in the back of the classroom, crying and holding her ear, too shy to tell her teacher because it was supposed to be quiet time. But Beth had noticed and had no qualms about interrupting the reading group. Mrs. Stokes had had Beth walk her down to the clinic where she stayed on a green leather cot, crying, until Trudy came to pick her up.

"Makes me not feel weird about you," Beth said.

Meg nodded. "My mother flew home that night. Even though it was a Wednesday."

"She always flew home when there was something wrong with you guys."

"Yeah." Meg lifted her legs onto the couch and wrapped her arms around her knees, remembering *that* night. After an emergency trip to the doctor, Trudy had tucked her into bed with soup and toast triangles, but Meg couldn't stop crying, even though her father had come home early from work. Then, suddenly, her mother was there, smelling of winter wind and perfume, gathering her up in a big warm hug while Meg cried and told her about how much it had hurt. Told her more than once. Then, Trudy brought up a big bowl of mashed potatoes—Meg's favorite food in those days—and she and her mother, who hadn't even taken off her coat, shared it, her mother saying funny things to make her laugh, Meg forgetting that she had ever had an earache.

Feeling self-conscious suddenly, she glanced over at Beth. "Uh, sorry."

Beth just shook her head.

"She was such a good Senator," Meg said quietly, then sighed. "I wish she'd stopped there."

CHAPTER FOURTEEN

Neither of them spoke for a while, looking at the movie.

"So what do we put in now?" Beth asked when *Gallipoli* ended. *"The Year of Living Dangerously?"*

Meg sat up. "Oh, uh, yeah. Whatever."

They watched the first part of the movie, still quiet.

"I don't know what to do," Meg said.

"About what?" Beth asked.

"Well," Meg grinned wryly, "everything, but I meant Josh."

"What do you *want* to do?"

"I don't know. I mean—" She shook her head. "I don't know."

"Well, I like Josh," Beth said. "I don't think you should blow it over something like this."

"Yeah, but—"

"So he didn't react exactly the way you wanted, so what? Let him have faults, why don't you?"

Meg frowned. "Being afraid of me is a pretty goddamn big one."

"It's a pretty goddamn *normal* one," Beth said. "I mean—" She drummed on the arm of the couch with one hand, then looked up. "Did it ever occur to you that you'd have a lot of these problems even if she *weren't* President?"

"Sure. She'd still be Senator."

Beth shook her head. "I mean if she weren't in politics at all. If she were—I don't know—a bus driver or something."

Meg had to smile, picturing her mother perched elegantly in the driver's seat, taking people to places she thought they would enjoy more than where they had asked to go. "A tight ship, but a happy one," she would say.

"It'd be *great* if she were a bus driver," Meg said aloud, imagining her mother sitting at the kitchen table at night, industriously polishing the badge on her Boston Transit cap, studying the transit code and route books so she would be able to speak intelligently about every facet of the MBTA.

"You're missing the point," Beth said, sounding impatient. "I mean—you're doing it right now."

Meg looked up. "Doing what?"

"Did it ever occur to you that you can be kind of hard to deal with?"

Meg frowned. "What do you mean?"

"Well, for one thing, you're always so busy thinking that people can't tell if you're thirty miles away, or listening to them, or what."

"I listen to people," Meg said uneasily.

"Sometimes."

Meg folded her arms, starting to get uncomfortable. "What else do I do?"

"You don't talk to people," Beth said without hesitating. "You get all upset about things, but you won't tell anyone about it, and you just walk around looking mean."

"My mother just got *shot*," Meg said. "Of course I'm upset."

Beth shook her head. "You do it all the time, Meg. You always have."

Meg looked at her for a minute, then scowled. "So I don't talk and I don't listen. Great." She moved her jaw. "That's just great."

"You're also touchy as hell," Beth said, then grinned. "It doesn't mean I don't like you."

"It's not like I'm the only person in the world with faults," Meg said defensively.

"Right," Beth nodded. "You have faults, I have faults, Josh has faults—maybe even Preston has faults." She paused. "Although I can't think of any." She glanced over. "And don't pretend like you didn't laugh because I saw you."

"I didn't," Meg said.

Beth just looked at her.

"Well, I didn't."

"Good for you," Beth said. "Talk about an iron will."

Meg tightened her arms across her chest, somewhere between laughing and giving her a smack. "You really make me mad, you know that?"

" 'That little Powers girl,' my mother used to say. 'Such a temper.' "

"She did not."

"Well—no," Beth admitted, and now Meg *did* laugh. "But I wouldn't have argued," Beth said quickly.

"You would have *encouraged* her, more likely." Meg slumped down into her sweatshirt, pulling the material up to cover the bottom half of her face. "I don't give *you* lectures."

"It's one of the things I like about you," Beth said, nodding. "Everyone *else* does."

Meg nodded. What with parents, and stepparents, Beth had probably gotten more than her share.

"Are you mad at me?"

"I don't know. Kind of." Meg sat up, taking her face out of the sweatshirt. "I don't know."

"You should just be—more receptive." Beth gestured around the room in general. "Don't use it as a crutch, you know?"

"Easy for *you* to say."

Beth nodded cheerfully.

"I'm *always* going to be the President's daughter," Meg said. "I mean, as long as I live. Me, and Margaret Truman, and Julie Nixon Eisenhower—"

"You're also the only person I know who's ever had lunch at Buckingham Palace," Beth pointed out.

Meg flushed self-consciously. "It was more like high tea."

"Will you listen to yourself?"

"I don't listen to *anyone*," Meg said.

"Oh, right, sorry. I forgot."

They looked at each other for a minute and finally, Meg grinned.

"Let's go get some lunch," she said.

Beth glanced at her watch. "It'll be more like high tea."

"You are *such* a jerk."

"I know," Beth said. "Good thing I'm beautiful."

Again, the White House arranged for Beth to be driven out to the airport and Meg stood outside the South Portico with her to say good-bye.

"Feel free to, you know, call me up sometime," Beth said. "Let me know what's happening."

"Well, I don't know." Meg looked around to see that there were at least five people within earshot. "If you can't manage to bring me more than a kilo, what good are you?"

"Hey," Beth shrugged expansively, "I did my best. If you start getting greedy, you're going to blow the whole thing."

"Yeah, well, you'd better do better next month," Meg said.

Beth nodded. "I'll talk to my people in South America."

"Good," Meg said. "Have your people call my people."

They both laughed, Beth adjusting the tilt of her hat.

"*Still* no photographers," she said sadly.

"Sorry." Meg shifted her weight. "Um, I'm glad you came."

Beth shrugged a "don't mention it" shrug. "Just keep it in mind when you're doing your Christmas list."

Meg laughed. "What a jerk."

"I know," Beth said. "I can't help myself."

After the car was gone, Meg went back into the house, running into Neal in the Center Hall.

"Hi," she said. "What's up?"

He stopped, looking at her accusingly. "How come me and Steven had to go to school and you didn't?"

"Because I'm the favorite," Meg said.

He scowled.

"That was a joke."

He just scowled.

"Look, I'm going to go take a shower. You and Steven get cleaned up too so we can be over at the hospital by five-thirty. And ask Mr. Collins to get some flowers together, okay?"

He nodded sulkily.

"Okay." She bent down. "Should I hug you, or am I too gross and ugly?"

He laughed, squirming away. "Too gross."

"Fine." She straightened up. "Your loss." She walked to her room, pleased to hear him laugh.

When they arrived at the hospital, their mother was just returning from a brief walk down the hall, surrounded by doctors and agents. Their father had his arm around her waist and she was leaning heavily on him, exhausted from walking the hundred feet or so. But when she saw them, she straightened up, smiling.

"Is it five-thirty already?" she asked.

They nodded.

"How do you feel?" Meg asked.

"Oh, much better." She had stopped leaning on Meg's father. "In fact—"

"Madame President, why don't we go into your room," Dr. Brooks said, "so I can check you over and then you all can have some privacy."

Her mother nodded and Meg knew that she had to be feeling terrible as she sank into the wheelchair a doctor rolled over.

"Don't I look silly?" she asked Neal, who giggled. She glanced at the rest of the family, smiling her politician smile. The politician smile always made Meg sad because her mother would use only her mouth, and her eyes would look terrible. Lonely, angry, depressed—whatever. In this case, fighting pain. "When I come home," her mother indicated the wheelchair, "I'll see if I can get two of these and then, we can have races." Meg's father was the only one who didn't smile and she lifted an eyebrow at him. "The image doesn't appeal to you?"

"It's a delightful image," he said.

"Thank you." She smiled at Meg and her brothers. "This will only take a minute," she said and let the doctors wheel her into her room.

Their father sat on a low couch. "Come here," he said. "Let's have some hugs."

Neal jumped in his lap and their father hugged him very tightly, Meg and Steven standing with their hands in their pockets. Their father gestured to the couch and they sat on either side of him.

"Beth get off okay?" he asked Meg and she nodded. "Good." He turned to Steven. "How about you? How was school?"

Steven shrugged. "You know."

"Me too," Neal said. He pulled on their father's tie and when he nodded, took it off completely. "Can Mommy come home? 'Cause she's walking around and everything?"

"Well." Their father hesitated. "It may be a few more days."

"This weekend?"

"More like next week, I think. But, we'll see." He shifted Neal so that he could see all of them. "Your mother's pretty tired today, so let's all be nice and quiet with her."

"What, you mean we have to go home?" Steven asked.

"No. I just meant to take it easy. Not to jump around or anything."

"Why would we do a jerky thing like that?" Steven wanted to know. "You think we're that stupid?"

"No. I'm sorry. I know you're not."

"Then why the hell do you keep telling us all the time?"

"I'm sorry." He put his arm on Steven's shoulders. Steven always picked fights at the hospital because he was afraid he would cry. When they were in her mother's room, he would slouch in a chair, fists clenched, not say-

ing anything, and more than once over the last week, he
had had to run out because he was crying.

"Quit looking at me," he said to Neal.

"I'm not," Neal said, looking at him.

"Dad, make him quit looking at me!"

"Shh," their father said gently. "Everything's okay."

"Oh, yeah." Steven stood up. "So okay she can't even
goddamn walk." He hurried down the hall, disappearing
into the men's room.

Meg's father sighed, starting to move Neal onto Meg's
lap.

"Don't!" Neal grabbed his arm. "Don't leave!"

"I'll go," Meg said, to avert a possibly noisy crisis.
She walked down the hall, frowning at the guards by the
men's room door. "Don't come in here," she said, then
knocked. "Steven? You in there?" Which was a pretty
stupid question. "I'm coming in, okay?" Slowly, she
opened the door and saw Steven sitting on the floor, below
the paper towel holder, arms around his knees.

"You're not allowed in here," he said.

"What are they going to do about it?" She sat next to
him, also wrapping her arms around her knees. Men's
rooms were colder and creepier than ladies' rooms. At
least, this one was. She didn't think she had been in any
others.

He was trying very hard not to cry, but it didn't work,
and he hid his face in his arms.

She rubbed his back. "Come on, it's okay."

"She can't even walk," he said, his voice choking.
"She can't even stand up."

"It takes a while to get better, that's all."

"Oh, right," he said bitterly. "So she can go outside
and have someone else shoot her?"

Meg rubbed his back. There wasn't much she could say
to that.

"It's not fair."

"No," she agreed. "It isn't."

"She should quit."

"She's President. The President can't just quit."

He didn't say anything.

"Well, she can't."

He still didn't say anything.

"Steven—"

" 'Cause she doesn't care about us. That's why."

"Steven, come on. You know that's not true."

He stood up, laboriously washing his face with a paper towel. "You gonna stay here and watch me go to the bathroom?"

She shook her head, also standing up. He kept his back to her and as she left, she heard a small sound, which meant that he was crying again. She kept going, not wanting to disturb his privacy, leaning against the wall outside to wait. He finally came out, his eyes red and his hair wet from having washed his face. She put her arm around him before he could say anything defensive, leading him down the hall to their mother's room. She released him at the door and they walked in, Meg with her arms folded across her chest, Steven's hands stuffed into his pockets.

"Hi," Meg said and Steven nodded.

"We were just talking about what to have for dinner," their mother said, all propped up, her eyes too bright.

"Whatever," Meg said and Steven shrugged.

"Here." Their father leaned over with a sparse menu. "Why don't you guys take a look at this?" He put his hand on Steven's shoulder, but Steven moved away from it.

Meg pretended to read the menu which, because her mother's diet was still restricted, was pretty dull, although the hospital was making an effort to at least *serve* the food beautifully. She sat back and closed her eyes, her head starting to hurt. If her mother wasn't talking or asking direct questions, no one really said anything. What a mess.

"I thought maybe Killington," her mother said.

Meg opened her eyes. "Killington?" She must have missed something.

"I thought, for a change, we might want to go there at Christmas. Unless you all would rather be at Stowe."

Meg looked at her doubtfully. Skiing? In less than two

months? This, from the woman who couldn't even walk down the hall and back?

"I'll be fine," her mother said. "I thought it might be nice to be in New England for a while."

"You mean, go home," Steven said instantly.

"For a while," their mother agreed.

So they talked about skiing, and every silence, no matter how brief, made Meg very uncomfortable. She'd always thought that the expression about air being thick enough to cut with a knife was stupid. Except that it was also accurate. Everyone talked about meaningless things while emotions flew around the room and smashed into each other. For a family of people she thought of as non-stop talkers, they sure were having trouble keeping a conversation going. And it was easy to let her mother do all the work.

It was like chess, sort of. Everyone watching everyone else, trying to figure out what move people were going to make next so they could set up the proper defenses. For that matter, it was like stupid *politics*. Even her mother, who was famous for her ability to manipulate audiences, couldn't make any of them relax or let down.

We're not much good as a family if we can only handle it when things are going well, Meg decided, and the sentiment seemed so appropriate that she almost said it aloud. But, why make things worse?

"You're awfully quiet tonight," her mother said.

"What?" Meg asked, startled. She looked around and saw that they were the only two in the room. "Where is everyone?"

"Clearing the trays away." Her mother frowned. "You didn't eat much."

"I had a big lunch." High tea, even.

"It was good for you to have Beth here."

"Yeah."

It was quiet again.

"I'm sorry," her mother said in a low voice.

"About what?"

"That I can't make it easier. I'm trying, but—" She

125

shook her head, her face the light gray color. "It'll be easier when I'm home."

And a target again.

"You all must be so angry at me," her mother said.

Meg waited for her to go on.

"You must feel as if I—" She swallowed and Meg watched the bones and tendons in her neck move— "I don't know. Asked for it."

The uncertainty in her expression made Meg feel guilty and she shifted in her chair. "No, I—I mean, we—I mean, just because you're President—well, you shouldn't have to worry about stuff like this. That's what's wrong."

Her mother touched her bandaged shoulder unhappily. "I never dreamed it would really happen. I never thought anyone—" She shook her head.

Meg didn't say anything, picking at some cat fur on her sweater cuff.

"I hated my mother for dying," her mother said, very quiet, and Meg started from the unexpectedness of the remark. It had happened when her mother was five, a riding accident, at the Connecticut farm her mother's family used in the summer. A real *Gone with the Wind* story, a case of a person taking a jump that was beyond her ability. "I really resented her for it," her mother said, speaking so quietly that Meg had to lean forward to hear her. "Leaving me like that."

"Well," Meg shifted, "she couldn't help it."

"I know that *now*," her mother said. "But when I was your age and younger, I always felt—" She stopped, looking right at Meg, who didn't meet her gaze. "I guess I thought that if she *really* loved me, she never would have done something that incautious. That, in a sense, she asked for it."

Meg flushed guiltily.

"Meg, I would never hurt any of you intentionally."

Meg nodded, eyes on her hands.

Her mother sighed. "I guess it's too late for that though, isn't it?"

Meg looked at the door. Where were her father and brothers? This was a very uncomfortable conversation.

"Meg?"

She glanced at her mother and away. "What?"

"It's all right to feel—"

Meg jumped up. "I'm going to see where Dad and those guys are, okay?"

Her mother nodded unhappily, seeming to crumple in.

"It's not that—I mean—"

The door opened and Meg's father came in, carrying Neal, who was crying.

"It's okay," he was saying soothingly. "You're okay now." Her mother looked at him and he nodded, her mother's eyes brightening. That meant that Neal had gotten sick again. He did that a lot lately. Her mother reached out with her good arm and her father lowered him gently onto the bed. She hugged him close, even though her face had stiffened with pain, whispering to him.

Steven was leaning against the wall, slouched and unhappy, and Meg went to lean next to him, just as slouched, her mother's low voice and Neal's crying the only sounds in the room.

CHAPTER FIFTEEN

Walking into school the next day felt strange—as if she had been away for years. People seemed afraid of her, the same way they had been when she had first started the January before: staring, then whispering as she passed.

There were Homecoming posters all over the place and she thought of Josh. He had been so cute the day he asked her to the dance, making a big deal of it—bowing low, giving her a white rose—even though it was pretty well understood that they would be going. Or, would have been.

She looked down the hall, seeing him at his locker. His shoulders looked sad. Slouched. Josh never slouched—he had grown about three inches in the last year and was pretty pleased about it.

Oh, hell, Beth was right. She started down the hall, towards his locker. But he was going the other way. Because he had seen her? She stopped. Okay, fine. If that was the way he wanted it. She turned and went to her own locker, irritated at him again.

She sat in English first period, looking at her book so she wouldn't have to meet eyes with anyone. She hadn't slept too well the night before and felt like resting with her head on her arms, but her teacher, Mrs. Hayes, probably wouldn't be too thrilled about that. But it would be nice to take a nap for a minute. She leaned her head on her hand, sliding her elbow until her arm was flat on the desk. That was probably as close to lying down as she could go without getting in trouble.

Then, as Mrs. Hayes discussed Gene Forrester's isolation in their book, *A Separate Peace,* someone knocked on the door. Meg—and everyone else in the class—sat straight up.

Oh, God, not again. Please, God, not again. Meg hung on to her desk with both hands, waiting for the bad news. Her parents, Steven, Neal—Mrs. Hayes crossed to the door, opening it.

"Of course, Carol," she said. "I think you left it on the back table."

Meg slouched forward, closing her eyes. It wasn't her family. Thank God it wasn't her family. She felt rather than saw the looks the rest of the class was giving the little tenth grader, who grabbed her notebook off the back table and hurried out. Meg took deep breaths, her heart feeling as if it were jumping all around her chest, caroming off her ribs.

"Well, now," Mrs. Hayes said. "Where were we?" She walked back to the front of the room, passing Meg's desk, touching her shoulder so swiftly that Meg almost didn't notice. Now she *did* rest her head on her arms, trying to calm down. It was just some kid, it wasn't—but maybe it meant that something bad *was* happening, that— she had to check.

She caught her teacher's eye, indicating the door. Mrs. Hayes nodded and Meg jumped up, almost running out. Her agents, on either side of the door, looked alarmed.

"Phone call," she said briefly.

They followed her down the hall, passing one of the patrolling agents on the way. She went to the alcove in the front lobby, pulling some change out of her jeans pocket. Holding her breath, she dialed the number and asked for her mother, the aide on the other end telling her that she was in a meeting.

"It's kind of important," Meg said, knowing that she had to hear her mother's voice before she could relax.

She was put on hold; then her mother came on.

"Meg?" She sounded worried. "Is everything all right? Where are you?"

"School." Meg let out her breath. Her mother *sounded* healthy. At least as if she were getting better. And she was obviously safe. Right now, anyway. "Are you okay?" she asked, to be sure.

"I'm fine."

"Is Dad okay?"

"He's fine. Meg, what's happening? Are you sure you're—"

"Yeah." She leaned against the side of the alcove, almost weak from the relief. "Steven—" She let out another breath. "Steven and Neal are probably okay too."

"Yes, they are." Her mother's voice was gentle.

"And you're *sure* you are?"

"I'm fine. Meg—"

"I have to go now," Meg said. "Sorry I interrupted you and stuff."

"Meg, wait a minute—"

"I just wanted to be sure you guys were okay. I, uh, I sort of have to go to class now."

"I love you," her mother said.

"Um, yeah, me too." Meg shifted her weight. "See you after school." She hung up, resting against the wall. When she felt under control, she straightened, opening the door. Intense fear was exhausting.

Back to English. She crossed the hall to the water fountain, splashing her face, some of the water soaking into her shirt and sweater. Too drained to worry about it, she started down the hall, stopping abruptly.

Josh was waiting against some lockers, his expression both nervous and concerned, his arms tight across his chest. They looked at each other, neither moving. Then, Meg walked over, leaning in for a hard, silent hug.

"Buy you a drink, sailor?" she asked against his ear.

He laughed, hugging her closer.

"I'm sorry," she said. "I've been a really terrible person lately."

"You're going through some pretty terrible things."

"Yeah, but—" She shook her head. "I'm sorry, Josh. I really am."

He hugged her even closer, not saying anything. For a minute, it was enough to be touching; then, it wasn't, and they were kissing about as hard as they had ever kissed, Meg not caring *who* was around to watch.

Behind them, someone cleared his throat. They broke just barely apart, turning to look. It was Mr. Carlisle, their physics teacher, his face stern, but also somewhat amused.

"Shouldn't you two be in class?" he asked.

They nodded, Meg too happy to blush.

"Then, maybe you ought to go," Mr. Carlisle said.

They nodded and he nodded back, continuing on his way.

"We probably can't risk that again," Meg said.

"Probably not," he agreed, much more flushed than she was.

She leaned up to kiss his cheek and they walked down the hall, holding hands.

"Are things any better?" he asked.

"I don't know." She sighed. "Not really."

"Will you let me help you?"

She leaned closer. "I'll try."

He nodded, tightening his hand.

When they were outside their English room, she stopped.

"Don't let me hurt your feelings," she said, "okay? I mean, if I take stuff out on you."

He flexed his muscles. "I'm tough."

She smiled. "Good."

He opened the door and it wasn't until she stepped inside that it occurred to her that their coming back together was going to be pretty obvious. Indeed, the entire class—including Mrs. Hayes—grinned and someone whistled the first few notes of "Reunited." This time, Meg blushed and Josh was the one who looked pleased. She sat in her isolated seat, Josh in his regular seat—she couldn't really move her books over during the middle of class.

"What, you don't even sit with him?" someone behind her asked.

"Matt," Mrs. Hayes said to him, "tell me what you think about the scene beginning on page thirty-two."

"Th-thirty-two?" He picked up his book, fumbling

through it, and Meg relaxed. That was two she owed Mrs. Hayes.

Having Josh nearby made things much easier and, even though she wasn't hungry, she sat at her regular lunch table. It was nice to be with a bunch of people who weren't wearing suits. Also people who talked about things like homework and "Hill Street Blues" and the Redskins. Normal things. She didn't really participate, but it was nice to listen.

Right after school, she went to the hospital. Her mother was in meetings most of the time and looked even weaker than she had the day before. But she and Meg's father were pretty happy because the doctors had decided that she could come home on Monday. Meg carefully didn't let herself think about the prospect of her being a target again.

Josh was coming over that night and Meg got home just in time to change. Since she had been so lousy, she sort of felt as if she should put out some effort. She wore her one pair of jeans which could never be described as being baggy and a gray cashmere sweater, along with a silver chain and appropriate small hoops. She put on lip gloss, some of her mother's Chanel No. 5, and even used some blusher to highlight her cheekbones. First-date time.

She sat on the staircase off the North Entrance Hall to wait.

"You look very nice," Arthur, the doorman, said.

"Thank you," Meg said shyly.

Josh was right on time and Meg stood up, not sure why she felt so shy. He had also taken some care dressing, and was actually wearing a tie underneath his sweater, and his charcoal gray pants which she personally thought were sexy as hell. His cheeks were red, but instead of a jacket, he had on a maroon tartan scarf. How jaunty.

"Hi," he said.

"Hi." She smiled nervously at Arthur. "See you later."

He nodded.

She and Josh walked upstairs.

"Wait a minute," he said, right before they got to the

132

top, and grabbed her in a hug. They kissed until they were out of breath, Meg hanging on to the railing with one hand to make sure they didn't fall down the stairs.

Josh moved back, straightening his glasses. "Hi."

She laughed. "Hi."

They ended up on the third floor, sitting on the couch in the Washington Sitting Room, neither of them saying much.

Meg let out her breath. "This feels kind of like the first time you came over."

He smiled. "I was scared to death that night."

"Yeah. Me too."

"*You* were?" he asked, sounding surprised.

"Well—yeah. I mean, of course I was."

"Yeah, but—why would *you* be scared?"

"I don't know." Meg picked up his hand, still feeling shy. "I mean, I didn't really know you and for all I knew you were—well, I'm not exactly great at trusting people."

"Yeah," he said wryly. "I've noticed."

She flushed, dropping his hand. "Are you mad at me?"

"You were mad at *me.*"

"No, I wasn't. I was just—" She sighed. "Mad."

"It didn't *seem* that way." He sighed too. "I don't know. Sometimes I wish—" He stopped.

"What?"

"I kind of wish I'd had a bunch of other girlfriends. Before you, I mean."

"To see if I measured up?" Meg asked stiffly.

"Meg."

"Yeah, well—" She heard Beth's voice saying, "You're doing it right now" and stopped. "What do you mean?" she asked, more pleasantly.

"Thank you," he said. "What I *mean* is—well, going out with you is kind of like—I don't know—running a marathon before you can *walk* or something."

Meg frowned. "I don't get it."

"Think hard," he said.

"Yeah, well, it's not my fault. I mean, I'm just normal."

"I just sometimes wish I'd started off with someone more my speed," he said.

"What, you mean I'm fast?"

He laughed. "Well, that's not *quite* what I meant."

She sat back, also grinning. "Do, um, I detect a note of irony there?"

"Let's just say 'fast' isn't the word I would have used."

"Oh, yeah?" She thought about that, then pushed him down, kissing him. She lifted herself onto her elbows, looking at him. "What word would you have used, Josh?"

He leaned up to kiss her. "Out of my league."

"That's four words." She kissed him back. "It's also stupid."

"Well, maybe." He took off his glasses and put them on the end table, blinking to focus. "Reporters bug me a lot. They call my house even."

Meg frowned. "I remember you told me about that guy from *People*, but I thought he was the only one."

He shook his head. "It happens a lot."

"You should have told me—Preston could probably do something."

Josh shrugged. "I just say 'no comment' mostly, or that they have the wrong number. Anyway, the thing is, they usually ask what someone like me is doing dating someone like you, and it's not all that dumb a question."

"Yeah, it is. And it's really rude too."

He just shrugged.

"Well, I'm sorry," Meg said. "I'll tell Preston to—"

"It's really not that big a deal," he said. "I only brought it up because—" He paused. "Actually, I kind of forget why I brought it up."

"You were failing to make a point."

"Oh. Right." He laughed suddenly. "You just said what I think you said, right?"

"I don't know, probably."

He laughed again, kissing her. "Mmmm," he said softly, moving to kiss her neck.

"I thought we were having a conversation."

"Later," he said, kissing her ear.

134

"The thing is—"

He sighed. "I bet you want to do *this* later."

"Well—yeah."

"Okay." He moved his hands behind his head, smiling up at her.

"Making yourself comfortable?"

"Yeah."

"Good." She rested her head on his shoulder. "The thing is, I need you to think that I'm normal, that—I mean, if you feel funny around me, it's like—" She sighed. "I don't know. I need to know that I can yell at you without—"

She shook her head.

"I didn't know what to do." He paused uneasily. "I *still* don't."

She turned her head to look at him. "You know what it is? Part of it—a lot of it, even—is *me* not trusting *you*, but *you* need to trust *me* too. I mean, you need to feel more secure about the whole thing. It's not like I'm going to run out and find some other guy—even if we have a fight. I mean, you have to trust me. All that matters is what *I* think, not what people try to make you *think* I think."

He nodded.

"Does that make sense, or is it stupid?"

"Both," he said.

She smiled. "That's what I figured."

"Mostly, it makes sense."

She nodded, and they were quiet for a minute.

"Well." He put his arms around her. "Enough conversation."

She laughed. "More than enough."

He left at around twelve-thirty, and going back upstairs, Meg couldn't hear any noise at all. Was it this quiet when her mother was home? It couldn't be.

Where was her father? Since it was so late, he had to be back from the hospital. Maybe he was asleep or—in case he wasn't, she knocked on her parents' bedroom door. There was no answer, so she walked down the hall to her own room. The door to the Yellow Oval Room was ajar,

135

even though it was dark inside, and she paused, then peeked in.

Her father was sitting on the couch, watching the low fire in the fireplace. Embarrassed by the idea of watching someone who didn't know she was there, she stepped back out into the hall, sitting down in a nineteenth-century chair to think.

She couldn't just go to bed and leave him there. But, if he wanted to be by himself, she didn't want to interfere with that either. Maybe—she walked down to the West Sitting Hall, then came back again, whistling aimlessly and calling Vanessa in a loudly hushed whisper that he would have to hear. Indeed, a small light went on in the room. She stuck her head in in a friendly way.

"Hi, Dad," she said. "I'm going to bed now."

He turned with a composed expression. Too composed. "Good night."

"Yeah." She put her hands in her pockets. "How was Mom?"

"Tired."

Meg nodded.

"Josh was here tonight?"

She nodded.

"Good," he said.

It was quiet.

"Well." Meg took a couple of steps towards the door. "Um, good night."

He nodded.

CHAPTER SIXTEEN

Meg spent most of the night before her mother came home in her room. Worrying. All the press could talk about was how important it was for a President to seem completely unafraid during that first public appearance. To give the country confidence and all. But that meant taking risks—smiling and waving a little longer, that sort of thing. Meg and her brothers were staying home from school so they could be there as soon as she got home, but her father wasn't letting them go to the hospital because, he said, the car would be too crowded. Meg knew that it was really because he didn't want to have to worry about them too.

Around eight-thirty, she put her book down, deciding to go see what her brothers were doing. She found them in the solarium with Kirby, looking subdued and sad, only half-watching the television. Trudy and her father were still at the hospital.

"Hi," she said.

They nodded.

Cheer them up. Think of something to cheer them up. "I came to see how my little peasants were doing." She tilted Neal's chin up, studying his face. "Although," she shook her head, "I had no idea that they were going to be such *ugly* little peasants."

Neal giggled, pulling his head away.

"I mean, good Lord." She patted Kirby. "This is the only decent-looking one in the bunch."

Her brothers laughed.

"You look just like us, Queenie," Steven said.

"Oh, God, no." She pretended to search for a mirror. "I can't possibly be *that* ugly."

"Don't kid yourself," Steven said.

"Well." Meg sat in between them even though there wasn't enough room. "I'm the Queen. I can get away with being ugly."

"Lucky for you," Steven said and Neal laughed.

"Are you going to watch TV with us, Meggie?" he asked.

"If you're not watching anything too queer." She squinted at the television, recognizing *Airplane II,* the VCR lights on. Videocassette companies had donated just about every movie they'd produced to the White House. "Looks pretty queer."

"How come you always laugh when you see it?" Steven asked.

"Well," she put a benevolent arm around each of them, "I like to keep my little peasants happy."

Neal laughed and Steven snorted, shrugging her arm off.

"Ah, yes," she went on. "Happy peasants. That's what I like to see. Lots of happy little—"

"If you want to make us happy, how about shutting up so we can watch the movie?" Steven asked pleasantly.

"When I can make you happier by sitting here and telling you swell jokes?"

"You tell *dumb* jokes," Neal said.

"What do you know about it?" Meg asked. "You're just a peasant."

"He got some book larnin' though," Steven said, watching the movie.

Meg laughed, giving him a quick hug.

"Do that again, chick, and you eat this." He showed her his fist.

"Oh, yeah, I'm real scared," she said.

"You best be, girl."

"Don't worry, munchkin, I am."

Their father came in. "I should have known you all would be up here," he said, putting on a parent smile, his eyes very tired.

"If it ain't the First Gentleman." Steven nudged Meg.

"He's got lots of book larnin'. Why don't you try some of your jokes on him?"

"Well, if you really . . ." Meg hung her head shyly.

"Yeah, go ahead."

"Well, okay, okay." She adjusted her position with some theatricality. "See, like, this funny thing happened to me on the way upstairs, right? I was like, walking by the Lincoln Bedroom, right? And this man comes out and says, 'Hey.' So I says, 'Hey what?' "

"Real quick of you," Steven said.

"Yeah, that's what I thought," Meg agreed. "Anyway, so he says to me, 'Meg,' he says—" She stopped, looking at her father. "What's the matter, don't you like my joke?"

"I love your joke," he said, his smile genuine. "Go on."

"Actually." She frowned. "I don't really know any jokes."

"At least you tried, Queenie," Steven said.

Their father looked both confused and amused. "You all seem pretty cheerful."

"Happy little peasants," Meg said. "How's Mom?"

"Busy packing her things. We'll be leaving the hospital at ten." He bent to be at Neal's level. "It's getting kind of late, pal. Think we ought to see about some bedtime?"

"But, the movie!" Neal pointed. "Can't I watch the movie?"

"The sooner you go to bed, the sooner you'll wake up and your mother will be here."

Neal yawned.

"Thought so." Their father picked him up. "Do you want to give your brother and sister a kiss good-night?"

Neal giggled and shook his head.

"Kiss me and you eat this." Steven held up his fist.

Neal giggled. "Night, ugly Queen," he said to Meg.

"Good night, ugly worm," she said.

It wasn't until later, much later when she was in bed, that she let herself worry again. The electric blanket was all the way up, Vanessa was asleep on her chest, but Meg was still cold. She kept picturing the scene: her mother leaving the hospital, arm wrapped up in the sling, smiling bravely and confidently at the crowd—and there would be a crowd. A huge crowd the stupid Secret Service wouldn't be able to do anything about. And in that crowd, there might be a person who—the phone rang and she flinched. When she answered it, the switchboard put her mother through.

"Hi," her mother said. "I'm sorry, did I wake you up?"

"No, I couldn't—I mean, I was awake. Is anything wrong?"

"No. Just doing some last-minute packing." Her mother paused. "Steven called me a little while ago."

"Yeah, he's sort of uptight about tomorrow."

"Well," her mother said. "I guess we all are."

Superwoman cracks slightly. *"You* are?"

"My God, Meg, what do you think?"

"I don't know, I—" Meg swallowed. "You aren't going to do anything—risky, are you?"

"Kiddo, I'm going to smile, wave and dive into the car."

"Dive?" Meg asked, the image almost amusing.

"In a manner of speaking." She let out her breath. "Nothing is going to happen, Meg."

"What makes you so sure?"

"I just am. We're all on edge because this is the first time I've been out in public, that's all."

"We're all on *edge* because you're important to us," Meg said.

"I know. I'm sorry."

"Sorry you're important to us?"

"No. I just—it really will be okay." Her tone changed abruptly. "So what are we going to eat tomorrow night? Pizza? Chinese food?"

"Are you allowed to have stuff like that?"

"I'm President, kid. I can do what I want."

Meg smiled. One of her mother's favorite lines. "I'm serious. Wouldn't it be better for us to have milk and

140

scrambled eggs and stuff like that?'' She laughed at the gagging sound her mother made. "I'm only being helpful."

"Let me put it this way," her mother said. "I'm not eating *any* more meals that don't require teeth."

"Hmmm," Meg said. "What an interesting way to put it."

"Let's just say I refuse." Her mother paused. "I really miss you. All of you."

"Um, yeah. We do too."

"Well." Her mother coughed. "I have to hang up now—they're bringing me lime Jell-O."

"Your favorite."

"That's what I said," her mother agreed. "I'll—see you in the morning."

"Yeah."

The plan was for her parents to come in through the North Portico; the press would be waiting there to "capture" the reunion. So, dressing as proper Presidential children, Meg wore a red plaid kilt with a V-neck sweater and white shirt; her brothers wore ties and their tweed jackets. Preston came upstairs to inspect them.

"Very nice," he said. "How about some smiles? You all look like you've forgotten how."

They smiled obediently.

"You've definitely forgotten how." He glanced around with exaggerated caution. "Okay." He reached into the inside breast pocket of his jacket. "If you all promise not to laugh, I'll show you something." He hesitated. "Do you promise?"

"We promise," Meg said, already grinning.

"How about you two?" He looked at Steven and Neal. "I mean, if this leaks, it could be very embarrassing. Can you keep a secret?"

Steven shrugged. "For a price."

"How about I catch bounce passes for a whole half-hour?"

"Sold," Steven said.

"Will you play pool with me?" Neal asked.

Preston nodded. "Half an hour."

"Okay, I promise," Neal said.

"Remember," Preston said, "you are the only three people in Washington, except for my optometrist, who know about this."

Meg laughed. "Optometrist, hunh?"

"Optometrist," Preston nodded, very grim. He sat on a yellow couch, taking an eyeglass case out of his pocket. "You see, I went in for my checkup a couple of weeks ago and look what I ended up with." He put on the stylish dark brown–framed glasses, looking very sad.

"Talk about *wimpy,*" Steven said.

Preston nodded. "I guess it's the end of my swinging bachelor life."

"Can I try them on?" Neal asked.

Steven decided that he wanted to try them on too and Preston let them, standing up and smiling at Meg. "What do you think?" he asked.

"Do you need them for reading?" She watched Neal strut around, the glasses slipping off his nose.

Preston nodded. "And it isn't bad enough for me to get contacts."

"I bet Dad'll fire you," Steven said, taking the glasses from Neal and putting them on. "He doesn't want any queer four-eyes working for him."

"Can't have any eggheads," Preston agreed. The phone outside the Yellow Oval Room rang and he picked it up, listening for a minute, then nodding. "Great, thank you. We'll be right down." He hung up. "We should go down now—the motorcade's just left the hospital."

"Um, without incident?" Meg asked, slipping into an automatic media phrase.

Preston smiled. "Without incident."

When the motorcade pulled up, agents jumped out, surrounding the presidential limousine. Her mother stepped out, smiling, her cheeks flushed with healthy color. Flushed with rouge, more likely, but she still looked good. She was wearing a sweeping wool cape instead of a winter coat—to minimize the sling, Meg figured. The press and staff broke into spontaneous applause.

"Thank you," her mother said. "It's great to be home."

"Can we go hug her now?" Neal whispered, trying to twist away from the hand Meg had on his arm. "Come on, Meg, let go."

"Okay, but be careful," Meg whispered back. "Don't hurt her side."

He nodded impatiently and she released him.

"Mommy!" He ran over.

"Hello, darling." Their mother bent awkwardly and Meg saw her father move closer, his hand on her back. Her mother kissed Neal, hugging him with one arm, then kissed and hugged Steven. Meg moved in for her turn, hearing cameras all around her. After the stagey reunion, they moved into the North Entrance Hall, Meg feeling like part of a five-member amoeba clump. There was more applause, her mother gave a short statement, and then her press secretary, Linda, allowed the reporters a few questions, most of which focused on her mother's health, her confidence level and her positions on gun control and the insanity plea. Her mother was light and relaxed—witty even, except on gun control and the insanity plea. On those two issues she was very serious, although actually, her positions were pretty much what they had been before the shooting. Only maybe now they meant more.

She noticed that her mother seemed to be trembling slightly, and Linda must have noticed too because suddenly her mother was striding over to the presidential elevator to go up to the family quarters. There was a wheelchair waiting in the elevator, but Meg was pretty sure that the press didn't know that.

She and her brothers took the stairs, meeting their parents outside the elevator where Trudy, along with most of the staff, was welcoming their mother back. Dr. Brooks was quietly steering her towards the bedroom, which was set up for convalescence. Meg saw that her mother was trembling more, even as she smiled and chatted with butlers.

"Madame President, I think it might be in your best interests to rest for a while," Dr. Brooks said.

"I think so too," her mother said and the staff faded away, returning to whatever they had been doing.

"In fact," Dr. Brooks said, "why don't we get you lying down so I can check your—"

Her mother was trembling visibly, her good hand gripping the arm of the wheelchair, the skin white. "I think I need to be by myself for a while," she said, her voice low.

"Okay," Dr. Brooks said. "First, why don't we—"

"I'm sorry, please excuse me." Her mother pushed out of the wheelchair and walked shakily into the Presidential Bedroom, shutting the door behind her.

Meg glanced at Steven and Neal, wondering if she looked as scared as they did.

"Your mother's been under a great deal of stress this morning," their father said, patting Steven, whom he was closest to, on the back. "Don't worry." He turned to Dr. Brooks. "Give us a while, will you, Bob?"

Dr. Brooks nodded, sitting on one of the couches, his bag on the floor next to him. The few aides who remained walked down the hall as though they had just remembered very important things they had to do.

Meg's father moved to the bedroom door, rapping gently. "It's only me, Katie," he said, and went inside, the door closing after him.

"What's wrong with her?" Neal asked, scared. "Is she crying?"

"Now don't you worry about a thing." Trudy took his hand. "She just needs a little privacy. Come on." She led him to the table in the hall. "You sit down with your brother and sister and I'll bring you all some hot chocolate." Hot chocolate. Trudy's panacea. That and Vick's Vaporub. "Dr. Brooks, would you like some coffee?" she asked.

"Thank you," he said.

Trudy returned with hot Danishes and cocoa for the

three of them, George bringing coffee for Dr. Brooks. The Danishes and cocoa were gone before the bedroom door opened. Meg's father came out, nodding to Dr. Brooks, who stood up, lifting his bag with him.

"Here, Russell." Trudy poured him some coffee and he smiled gratefully. "They're warming some milk for Katharine."

He nodded. "Thank you."

"Gross," Steven commented.

Meg elbowed him. "Shut up, you little brat."

"It's all right, Meg," their father said. "He has a point."

"Can we see Mommy?" Neal asked.

Their father pulled out his handkerchief to wipe off Neal's chocolate mustache. "As soon as Bob's finished," he promised, slipping the hanky back into his pocket. "Remember, you still have to be very careful. Especially if you get on the bed."

"We know, Dad," Steven said, sounding irritated.

"It's just a reminder." Their father indicated Neal with his eyes. "And watch Kirby."

Kirby, lying on the floor, wagged his tail. Trudy bent to straighten the red Welcome Home ribbon he was wearing on his collar.

"You know." She stood up. "I believe I'll go upstairs for a while."

Neal looked worried. "Are you sick?"

"Of course not." She straightened his hair with the same motion she had used to fix Kirby's ribbon. "I just think you all ought to have some time together." She winked at Meg's father, gave them each a hug, and left.

When Dr. Brooks came out, they went in, Meg feeling very formal. Their mother was propped up by pillows and even though it was obvious that she had washed her face and reapplied her makeup, Meg could tell that she had been crying. Now, however, she was smiling, and Adlai and Sidney were curled around her legs. Kirby came in, tail wagging, and Steven grabbed him before he could bound onto the bed.

"Hello, Kirby," their mother said cheerfully. "Steven, don't worry about him. Come on." She patted the bedspread, and Kirby climbed onto the bed, large and clumsy.

"Kate." Meg's father was immediately at her side.

"I'm fine. I won't break." She smiled at Neal. "Come sit with me, I'm lonely."

Neal beamed, scrambling across the blankets to sit next to her, larger than Kirby and only slightly less clumsy. Meg looked at Steven, who had his arms across his chest and one of his unreadable expressions that she was pretty sure meant worry. George came in with the hot milk and her mother frowned as though confronted by a particularly challenging puzzle, her good arm around Neal and unavailable to accept the mug.

"Thank you, George," she said. "Just put it there," she inclined her head towards her bedside table, "and I'll have some in a minute."

Problem solved. No wonder she was the President. Meg sat on the sofa by the fireplace, wondering why no one in the room seemed to know how to act. She sure didn't. It would have been easier if Trudy had stayed. Her father was jittery: sipping coffee, putting the cup down, picking it back up again. Steven was rocking on his heels, not saying anything, and Neal was just smiling and playing with their mother's hand.

"Well," their mother said. "This is rather like a wake."

Meg jumped, Steven rocked, their father frowned.

Meg stared at her hands, twisting her fingers into different contortions. What was everyone else thinking? She had pictured the President in bed, in her lounging gown, the family gathered around her, everyone being very loving. Instead, silent tension.

"Have we all had breakfast?" her mother asked.

"Twice," Steven said.

More silence. Meg made her hands into a church with a steeple, then opened them to see all the people. Why didn't someone make a joke? If only she could think of one.

"Look," her mother said, "I'm sure all of you would rather—"

"What, you don't want us in here?" Meg asked, surprised by the hostility in her own voice.

"Darling, of course I want you in here," her mother said patiently. "It's just—well, I don't know. You all seem so uncomfortable." She blinked a few times, lifting her arm away from Neal long enough to pick up her mug and drink some milk.

"Are you tired?" Meg's father asked. "Would you like to rest for a while?"

"I just got up, Russell." Her mother sounded somewhat testy and the waves from this parental exchange moved through the room, making Meg even more uncomfortable.

"Well, hell." Steven jammed his hands into his pockets, his voice grumpier than either parent's. "You wanna play Monopoly or something?"

Meg laughed, relieved that someone had finally said something funny, and her parents smiled.

"I like Monopoly," Neal said happily. "Can I be the car?"

"*I'm* being the car," Steven said.

"What if I want to be the car?" their mother asked. "I get tired of being the shoe all the time."

"I assume that's a joke," their father said, "since I'm the one who's always the shoe."

"Yes, Russell, it's a joke."

"Well, good." He smiled. "Because I'm the biggest and this time, *I'm* being the car."

"I don't care," Steven shrugged. "I call being the dog."

Meg stood up. "Where's the set? In the solarium, or what?"

"Meg, don't bother," her mother said. "George or someone can bring it."

Meg shrugged and sat down.

147

"What's Meg, anyway?" Neal asked. "The thimble?"

"Yeah," Steven nodded. "She's always the thimble."

"I'm always the dog, jerkhead," Meg said from the couch. "You're lucky I'm giving you a turn."

"Oh yeah," Steven said. "Real lucky."

"Will you all stop bickering?" their father asked, on the phone.

"So speaketh the proverbial pot," their mother said.

"Katharine," he said, amused, "if being the car means that much to you, I'll—" He returned to the phone. "Thank you. Just bring it to our bedroom, please." He hung up, smiling at the family. "Okay, who's going to be banker?"

CHAPTER SEVENTEEN

Meg got to be banker. She was always the banker. They played for about two hours, everyone being much better sports than usual, breaking the game up when lunch was served, which Meg noticed was easily digestible pasta. So much for pizza and Chinese food.

Politically speaking, it was amusing to watch her mother play: her technique was to buy up all of the low-income land, like Baltic and Mediterranean Avenues, cover them with expensive housing, and make a killing. Kind of like what they did in Boston, and Meg remembered the Senator—her mother—speaking out against this practice in the past. Luckily, her mother never played Monopoly in public.

Neal was annoying to play with—he would buy St. James Place and Ventnor Avenue and then refuse to give up the pretty colored cards, spoiling anyone else's chances for monopoly. In her family, whenever anyone landed on the income tax square, they would automatically give up the two hundred dollars without bothering to figure out their assets since her father got such gleeful joy out of totaling them up and assigning debts. Once a tax attorney, always a tax attorney. Steven spent his time trying to get the dice to fall just right so he would land on Free Parking and get to take all the money from the middle of the board.

Meg, on the other hand, was a very subdued player. She would buy every single piece of land she could and then, hoard them, waiting for someone to say, "Hey, who has Kentucky Avenue?" As banker, she was able to keep mental track of how much money everyone else had and she would ask incredibly high prices for the desired property, which the greedy land buyer—often her mother—would pay, and then be too bankrupt to put any housing on it. Her mother was always having to cash in hotels and spread her wealth more sensibly. Meg would take half of whatever she earned from sales and collecting two hundred dollars as she passed Go, and put it under the board where she wouldn't spend it. Then, at key moments of the game, when a member of her family was just about to go under financially, she would pull out some of the hoard and offer outrageous prices for the person's property. Little knowing how much money Meg still had hidden, the person would accept the overwhelmingly generous offer; Meg would acquire another monopoly, and by investing more of her savings in housing, win back the fortune she had paid for the land in no time. She liked playing Monopoly.

"Well, let's see," her father said, finishing figuring out assets as the rest of the family finished lunch. "It looks as if Meg has just nudged you out, Katharine."

Her mother frowned. "How much?"

"Four thousand, six hundred and eighty-six dollars."

"It's because of the damn money she hides under the board," Steven said, his mouth full of garlic bread.

"It's 'cause she steals from the bank," Neal said. "I see her do it."

Meg put down her fork, offended. "I don't steal. I just plan ahead more carefully."

"You just *cheat* more carefully."

"What's this you're saying?" Meg lowered an eyebrow at him. "You cheat?"

"I do not!"

"Well, wait." Meg pretended to be perplexed. "If I cheat *more* carefully, the only conclusion I can make is that *you* cheat *less*—"

"Meg, leave him alone," their mother said. "I'm sure that neither of you cheats." She frowned. "Although that money trick of yours *is* a little sneaky."

"Don't knock it," Meg's father said, shrugging. "Every Administration needs a fiscal wizard."

"Yeah," Meg's mother said wryly, "and I'm stuck with one who's underage."

Meg grinned. It was nice to hear her family bickering.

Her mother glanced at her watch. "Well, it's almost two and I think it's about time to get some work done."

"You're not getting out of bed," Meg's father said quickly.

"Not today," her mother agreed. "That, however, does not preclude work." She reached awkwardly onto her bedside table, moving the phone onto the bed. As she spoke to members of her staff, setting up afternoon meetings, Meg watched her turn into the President, a change she hadn't seen very often lately and was now aware that she hadn't missed. Her mother paused, glancing at Meg's father, who didn't look very happy about the change either. "Darling, I have to," she said.

He sighed, but nodded, reaching across the bed to take Neal's hand. "Come on, guys," he said. "Let's go do something athletic."

"Don't you have to be the First Gentleman?" Steven asked, checking before he got excited.

"Not today I don't," their father said firmly, and Meg wondered if that was meant to be a criticism of her mother. Probably not a conscious one. "Let's go shoot some baskets and Brannigan can get some nice pictures out of it."

Mike Brannigan was the White House photographer who was supposed to follow them around the family quarters and at Camp David and everything to take informal pictures. Once he caught Meg leaving her bedroom on her way to get the book she had left in the West Sitting Hall, her face covered with Noxema. He had also taken pictures of her swimming in the White House pool, and trying to find a place to sunbathe on the roof early last April during an unexpected heat wave. Meg had complained to her parents, who decided that rather than having evil intentions, Brannigan was simply in the habit of taking pictures of *everything* the First Family did. Her mother had given him the firm suggestion that he exercise a little more decorum, particularly in the presence of adolescent women. It was Meg's opinion that he was a closet lecher, given to constant secret fantasies. When she broached this to Steven, he said, "Yeah, you only wish," and since then, Meg had kept this opinion to herself. She also spent a couple of months checking around corners and behind doors, much to the amusement of the staff. But after her mother's warning, Brannigan had confined himself to appropriately chaste pictures of Meg walking Kirby on the South Lawn, studying at the black walnut table in the Treaty Room, and making popcorn with Steven and Neal. Meg still didn't trust him, and if her father coerced her to shoot baskets, would be certain to wear something shapeless like her old I Love Boston sweatshirt, even older gray sweat pants, and in all probability, an ancient terry-cloth hat. The hat was the epitome of tacky, and by no means flattering, but she would far rather be frumpy than self-conscious.

"You going to play with us?" Steven asked.

"Why don't you," her mother said before Meg could answer. "Get some color in your cheeks."

Meg was going to sigh long-sufferingly and say, "All right, if I *have* to," the way she normally would, but rather than start trouble, she smiled brightly and said that she would be delighted. Enchanted.

She shot baskets for almost an hour at the hoop the landscaping staff had erected near the Lyndon Johnson Children's Garden. Another narrow and secluded place had been converted to a baseball pitching area where Steven had convinced the gardeners to make him a regular mound and home plate. Probably not a permanent addition to the White House grounds. The staff at Camp David had gone all out, making him a perfect place to practice.

Outdoor activity felt good, but Meg found that she got tired pretty quickly. Frightening how easy it was to get out of shape. Time to get back out on the tennis court. Steven and her father gave every indication that they were going to play all afternoon, and Neal was doing his stubborn best to keep up with them. Meg, tired of playing and tired of having her picture taken, moved to the sidelines, deciding to go wander around the Jacqueline Kennedy Garden or bang on the piano in the East Room. To call her repertoire limited was less than an understatement, although Josh sometimes taught her simple tunes. Very simple. She wanted to learn "Rhapsody in Blue" or the "1812 Overture," but he taught her things like Christmas carols and the Pink Panther theme.

"How about one more?" Mike Brannigan said, pointing his camera from the far end of the court. "Why don't I take one of you wiping your face with that towel?"

"Why would I wipe my face?" Meg asked. "I'm not perspiring."

"Meghan doesn't perspire," Steven said solemnly. "She glows."

"Right," Meg said. "You, on the other hand," she snapped a hard pass at him, "sweat."

"Yup," he agreed, trying a hook shot that just barely hit the backboard. "You only wish you were a guy so you could too."

Meg nodded. "I confess." She picked up the towel without thinking, blotting her face, and heard the camera click.

"Thanks, Meg," Mike Brannigan said. "Good shot."

She blushed, putting her terry-cloth hat back on. "See you guys later," she said to her father and brothers, then nodded politely to everyone else before wandering away, her agents behind her. God *forbid* they let her walk across the backyard by herself.

Preston, who had been watching them play and taking an occasional shot himself, caught up with her. "Heading for the house, kid?"

"I guess so."

"Me too."

They walked on the cement oval surrounding the central part of the South Lawn, passing the Jimmy Carter Cedar Tree of Lebanon. Her mother didn't have a tree yet. She had some roses though.

"How you feeling, kid?"

Meg shrugged. "Kind of tired. I guess I'm out of shape."

"No, I meant about today. Having your mother home."

"Oh. Well, I'm glad."

He nodded. "Me too. Things are okay with old Joshua?"

She blushed. "Yeah."

"Good."

They walked along and he kicked a dried leaf the gardeners had somehow missed raking up. Off with their heads.

"I've had a couple of phone calls from *Seventeen,*" he said.

Meg scuffed her Tretorns along the cement, looking for a leaf of her own to kick. "How come?"

"Because of everything, they want to extend your interview, or at least change the focus a bit. I told them it would be up to you and your parents." He glanced at her. "What do you think?"

Meg scuffed harder. "What did Dad say?"

"I thought, in this case, that it might be better to find out your opinion first."

"What do they mean, 'extend the interview'?"

"It means that you'd have to answer a lot of difficult, and potentially very painful, questions."

"Oh," Meg said, her face tightening. "You mean like, 'How does it feel to have some maniac blast away at your mother with a rifle?' "

He nodded. "Phrased somewhat more delicately."

"What if I don't feel like talking about it?"

"That's your prerogative."

Meg sighed, sitting on the steps leading up to the South Portico. "What do *you* think?"

"That you should think it over, then discuss it with your parents."

"They'll probably say it's up to me."

"Probably." He sat next to her.

"What would *you* do?"

"I think I'd extend the interview."

Meg frowned. "Why?"

"Well, it'll give you a chance to say what *you* think, in your own words, and they won't have to write their own version. Think about it, Meg. If they don't mention it at all, the article won't make much sense."

"What if it had happened the day before the magazine was printed? Would they stop the presses?"

"No. But it didn't happen the day before."

"Yeah, but what if—"

"Don't talk 'what ifs,' " he said. "They're never worth much, but in the White House, they're pointless."

Meg couldn't come up with an answer to that.

"It happened, it's history, and you have to go from there."

Meg folded her arms.

"Look, kid. It's inevitable that they're going to write *something*. Wouldn't you feel better having some control over it?"

She shrugged.

"I'm sure you would." He grinned. "Seeing as I know how much you hate having people put words in your mouth."

Meg acknowledged the joke with a half-smile.

"In the long run, I think it might make things easier for you," he said. "The more you talk about it, the faster you're going to be able to get over it."

"Get over it," Meg said.

"Get over with it. Deal with it. All those things." He lifted his hand from her shoulder to adjust her hat. "You know what I mean?"

She nodded.

"You want to talk about it?"

She shook her head.

"Want to come hang out in my office?"

"No, thanks," she said. "I think I'm going to go play the piano."

"Still learning 'Hill Street Blues'?"

She nodded.

"Keep up the good fight," he said and they both stood up.

CHAPTER EIGHTEEN

They had thick corn chowder for dinner, and dessert was a choice of puddings: chocolate, butterscotch and rice. No tapioca. Downer. Trudy took Steven and Neal downstairs to watch *Return of the Jedi*—her brothers begged for Star Wars movies almost every week—and Meg sat through part of it with them. But she had seen it about ten times, so she went upstairs to see what her parents were doing.

When she knocked, there was no answer, and just as she walked away to go look for them, her father said, "Come in." Meg opened the door uneasily, not sure what she might have interrupted. Her father was sitting on the couch, reading *The Post;* her mother was in bed, going through papers and reports, the telephone on her lap.

"I, uh—" She put her hands in her pockets, uncomfortable. "I'm going to go read for a while, so I thought I'd say hi."

Her parents nodded.

"Is everything all right downstairs?" her mother asked.

"Yeah, they're watching the movie." She glanced from one parent to the other. Maybe she'd walked in on an argument or something. It *was* kind of strange that her father was on the couch instead of the bed. "Well, I'll probably say good-night now—in case I fall asleep or something."

"You look tired," her mother said.

"Kind of. Does, um, Kirby need to go out?"

"Brian just took him," her father said. "I'll take him again before I go to bed."

"Oh. Okay." Meg backed up. "Well, good night." It occurred to her that she should have hugged her mother and she came back in, hugging her clumsily, trying not to hurt her shoulder or side. Then, she went over to hug her father, not wanting to play favorites.

"Preston tells me that *Seventeen* wants to come back," he said as she straightened up, and her mother stopped reading.

Meg nodded. "They want to extend it."

"Update it?" her mother asked.

"I guess." Meg didn't look at her, afraid to see her expression. "They said it's up to me. And you guys too," she added quickly.

"Do you want to do it?" her father asked.

"Well." Meg pushed her hair over her shoulders. "I don't really think it's necessary."

"I rather expect it is," her mother said. "It will seem ridiculous otherwise."

Meg checked her expression before answering—it was more blank than anything else. Her face was tight, but it had been that way ever since it happened. She sure looked older though. For the first time—probably ever—her mother, who exercised constantly and used so much Oil of Olay that she was probably a major stockholder in the company, looked her age. Looked older than her age.

"I think it might be a good idea," her mother said.

"You mean, I have to?"

"You don't *have* to. It just seems sensible to me." She glanced at Meg's father. "Don't you think so?"

"No," he said.

"Well," her mother began, "I really think—"

"Why put her through it again?" he asked. "That woman gave her a terrible time."

"In this situation, I'm sure she wouldn't—"

"How do you know?" he asked. "My God, Kate, she's having a rough enough time as it is. Why make it worse?"

Meg drifted uneasily towards the door, not wanting to be part of, or a witness to, this argument. Her parents never fought. At least, not in front of her. This was a lousy time to start.

"I'm *trying* to make it easier," her mother said through clenched teeth.

Her father started to say something, glanced at Meg and abruptly left the room. Meg kept her eyes down, embarrassed.

"I *have* to get back to work," her mother said defensively.

Meg tilted her head, confused, then caught on to the fact that maybe her parents were arguing about something other than the interview. "Well, sure," she said. "I mean, if you're well enough."

"I'm fine," her mother said and it sounded so familiar, so false, that Meg didn't respond, concentrating on the way her Topsiders curled up in the front. Like elf shoes. She leaned back on her heels, making them curl up more.

"Would you mind leaving me alone?" her mother asked, her voice oddly blurred.

Meg looked up. "Alone?"

Her mother nodded, face turned away, good hand up at her eyes, and Meg saw that she was crying.

"Mom?" She approached the bed. "Wouldn't you rather that I—"

"No! Just leave me alone."

Meg backed up towards the door, guilty and worried. "I'm sorry," she said and hurried out. Too rattled to go into her room, she went to the East Sitting Hall, planning on going to the Treaty Room to sit and stare at the chandelier. But, it was getting late, and with her luck, Lincoln's ghost would show up. She veered left at the Yellow Oval Room, opening the door to go in and maybe stand out on the Truman Balcony to look at the Washington Monument. But her father was at the window already, hands in his pockets, back to her. She was going to say something, thought better of the idea, and closed the door. Maybe, just this once, she would risk Lincoln's ghost.

"What do you expect?" Josh asked as they sat in the

library during their study period. "When people are up-set, they get in fights."

She blushed. "Not everyone's that much of a jerk."

"It doesn't make you a jerk—it's normal."

"That doesn't make it any better."

He reached out to move some hair away from her face, Meg leaning her cheek against his hand. "He's worried about her. Of course he's upset."

"But, she's hurt. You can't yell at someone who's hurt."

"What, you're going to wait until she's better?"

"No, I—" Meg frowned. "Aren't you listening to me? I'm talking about my father."

He nodded.

"Oh," she said. "You're trying to make me do a Freudian slip or something."

"I just get the feeling you're mad at her."

Meg shrugged. The night before, she *had* been really mad at her. After her parents' argument, and sitting in the Treaty Room for an hour, staring at the chandelier, she had gone to her room, climbing into bed to watch the news. Naturally, her mother was the top story and they showed a film of the President leaving the hospital. She came out, the bluish gray cape swinging in the wind, and instead of the quick wave and jump into the car she had promised, she stood there without moving or smiling, as if daring someone to shoot her. Meg had watched, both angry and proud—mostly angry—as agents swarmed closer and her mother still didn't move, studying the crowd. Then, with a brief nod to the press, and an even briefer wave, she strode to the car, relieved agents crowding her inside. Meg had turned off the television after that, lying in the dark-ness, so angry at her mother for taking stupid chances that her fists clenched under the blankets. How many people would have the courage to walk out after being shot and dare someone to do it again? Only, why did it have to be *her* mother? Why couldn't it be someone else's mother? *Anyone* else's mother.

"Meg?" Josh asked.

She looked up.

"Would you rather talk about something else?"

"No." She sighed. "I don't know."

"We can if you want."

"Did you see the news last night?"

He nodded.

"Did you see her leaving the hospital?"

He nodded.

"That was really selfish," Meg said. "Her doing that, I mean."

"It was *brave*," he said.

"With three kids at home, afraid someone's going to hurt her, and they'll never see her again?"

He folded his arms on the table, leaning over them. "Would you rather she had come out, burst into tears, and run to the car?"

Meg looked at him, both amused and irritated. "No," she said.

"So it could have been worse."

"Yes. It could have been worse."

He started to say something, then stopped. "Do you want to talk about something else?"

"Yes."

"Well." He blinked several times. "Then we will."

"Not uptight or anything, are you?"

He nodded sheepishly. "I don't want to upset you."

"What about everyone else?"

"What do you mean?"

"I don't know. No one's really talking to me lately."

Josh shrugged. "It's a weird situation. People don't know how to handle it."

"That's for sure." She slouched forward, head on her arms. "Do you mind if I rest?"

He squeezed her shoulder, keeping his hand there. "No."

She closed her eyes, very much wanting to sleep. Another hand came onto her back, this one clumsier.

"You, uh, okay?" Nathan asked awkwardly.

She lifted her head. "Yeah. Fine."

He nodded, moving his hands into his pockets. "This private?" he asked, indicating the two of them.

"No," Meg said. "It's not private."

He turned. "Yo, Zack," he said across the library and Zachary came slouching over from the magazine rack, his pen in his mouth like a cigarette. They stood awkwardly, not sitting down, both the same height, Nathan at least fifty pounds heavier. Kind of an amusing contrast.

"You going to stand there all day?" Josh asked and they sat down, the way they moved reminding Meg of Kirby.

No one said much of anything.

"What's with Alison?" Meg asked, scanning the library and locating her in a carrel, doing homework.

Zack and Nathan looked at each other.

"Feels bad," Zack said. " 'Bout tennis and all."

"Yeah, but that wasn't—" Meg sighed. "Be back in a minute." She walked over to Alison's carrel, hands automatically going into her pockets. Awkwardness seemed to be the name of the game. "Um, you busy?"

Alison looked up, chic in her oversized shirt, skinny leather belt and scarf made of two bandannas braided together, one blue, one pink. "No," she said, closing her book.

Meg nodded, pulling a chair over, sitting with one knee up, arms wrapped around it. "I'm sorry. I've really been a slime lately."

"N-no," Alison said. "You haven't—"

"Oh, come on. I've been terrible."

"No," Alison said. "A little—withdrawn, maybe."

Meg laughed. "A little."

Alison laughed too. "Okay, completely."

"Now *that's* more like it." Meg sat back, lifting her feet onto the chair at the next carrel. "Are you going to support my nomination to the Phone Call Returners Club?"

"No."

Meg laughed again. "Good for you." She glanced over. "What happened at the match yesterday?"

Alison looked guilty. "We won four-three."

"Hmmm," Meg said, then grinned wryly. "I kind of almost wish everyone had been so demoralized that you'd lose."

"Mrs. Ferris gave us a 'Do it for Meg' speech."

"She did not."

"Well—no," Alison agreed.

"Didn't think so." Meg frowned across the library at her agents. "If they let me, I'll come watch tomorrow."

Alison nodded uncomfortably.

"Don't feel guilty, okay? It's my stupid agents' fault, no one else's."

"Are there—other things you aren't going to be allowed to do?" Alison asked, still looking uncomfortable.

"Probably, I don't know." Meg shrugged. "Whatever." She looked over. "How are *you?*"

"Well—fine."

"Is your brother still dropping out?"

Alison grinned wryly. "Yeah. He says he's going to Colorado to teach skiing."

"I may join him," Meg said.

"That'd make some headlines."

"Yeah, really. What do your parents think?"

Alison just shook her head.

"Bad scene."

"Yeah," Alison said. "It's pretty stupid—he only has one semester left after this, but he says he doesn't want to miss spring powder."

Meg laughed. "He has a point."

"Good old Josephine Skier," Alison said.

"Yup, that's me."

Alison nodded, her expression amused, then sobering. "Meg, is there anything I can *do?*"

"No. I mean, thanks, but—I don't know. It seems like my family's just going to have to"— she was going to say "fight," but changed her mind—"figure it out. I don't know."

"Okay, but if there is—"

Meg nodded, studying her for a minute. For some reason, she had always attracted snappily dressed friends.

Rather an interesting contrast. "I sure hope I dress better next time," she said aloud.

Alison looked blank.

"Next life," Meg elaborated. "I could use some style." She glanced over at Josh and Nathan and Zack, all of whom were visibly restless. "Want to go over there and—I don't know—be rowdy or something?"

Alison grinned. "You mean, try to get kicked out?"

"Yeah." Meg also grinned. "What the hell."

Talking to people made things easier at school, but they still weren't so great at home. Her mother didn't seem to be getting better and could only work for an hour or two at a time, at which point she would practically collapse. Her father was tense and worried, drinking far too much coffee, and either angry at her mother for working too hard, or fiercely protective. Trudy was trying to do everything at once—be there for Meg and her brothers, take care of her mother, comfort her father. Steven slouched a lot; Neal sat next to whichever parent was in the room, panicking if neither was available.

Meg spent most of her time trying to stay out of the way. Trudy spent hours with her mother and Meg would see the two of them walking up and down the second floor hall, her mother leaning a little less each day. The two of them sitting on a couch, Trudy talking in a low voice, her mother nodding unhappily. Sometimes they weren't talking at all and Trudy would just be rubbing her mother's shoulder. A couple of times, it was obvious that her mother had been crying. If Meg saw them, she would veer the other way, not wanting to disturb their privacy.

Coming home from school one afternoon, she went upstairs, passing Steven dribbling in the North Entrance Hall. Since—everything, her parents had lifted the in-house dribbling ban.

The door to the Presidential Bedroom was ajar and Meg checked to see what was going on before entering. Trudy was straightening her mother's blankets and fluffing her pillows while her mother, surprisingly docile, watched her do it.

"Here, drink some of this," Trudy said, handing her mother a mug from the bedside table. "It will make you feel better."

As her mother sipped some of whatever the liquid was, Meg knocked hesitantly on the door.

"Um, can I come in?" she asked.

"Of course," her mother said. "How was school?"

"Okay. How do you feel?"

Her mother smiled a little politician smile, which meant lousy. Meg came all the way into the room, curious enough to lean over and see what was in the mug. It looked like tea. Very pale tea.

"Lemonade," her mother said.

"*Hot* lemonade?" Meg asked, the concept disgusting.

"There are those who find it delightful," her mother said.

"Apparently so," Meg said, adopting the same tone of voice. "You want me to go put on a Victorian dress?"

Her mother just sipped the lemonade, which actually smelled pretty good.

"Can I try some?" Meg asked.

"Ha," her mother said.

"Well." Meg stepped back. "So, you, uh, feel better?"

"I think so," her mother said, sounding doubtful. "I was able to work most of the morning."

"She's *much* better," Trudy said. "We walked for a good half-hour this afternoon."

"Outside?"

"Well, let's not get carried away," her mother said.

Trudy touched her shoulder. "It's going to be gradual, Katharine. Recovering from *any* injury is."

Her mother nodded, suddenly looking so unhappy that Meg backed towards the door.

"I, uh, guess I'll be in my room," she said. "I mean, if anyone wants me."

In her room, she picked up *Chilly Scenes of Winter*, a book by Ann Beattie, and got into bed, pausing only to pat Vanessa.

"So, what's up?" she asked, patting her under the chin, which her cat adored. "You watch 'All My Children' today? Oh, yeah? Well, what did I miss?" She kissed the top of her cat's head and opened her book. Nothing like a little private whimsy. Especially with cats. Vanessa had a fine appreciation of whimsy.

"Hi," Neal said, standing just beyond her threshold. He was very respectful of other people's rooms, probably because Steven was a big one for personal space and terrorized anyone who came in his room without permission.

Meg lowered her book. "Hi. School okay?"

His shrug was a blatant imitation of Steven's "I'm thirteen, I'm cool" shrug. Neal was hitting a macho period and, looking at him in old sneakers, rumpled jeans and blue sweater, with his shirt untucked and half of his collar sticking out, she smiled. He was even starting to *dress* like Steven.

"You want to talk to me," she asked, "or are you too cool to hang out with girls?"

He giggled. "You're my *sister.*"

"Sorry. I forgot."

He came over to the bed, climbing up next to her. "Mommy's still sick in her room."

"Yeah, I know."

"Will she be okay soon?"

"I hope so." Meg ruffled her hand through his hair. He needed a haircut. That was one easy way to see how awful her mother was feeling—normally, she would never let him walk around looking shaggy. It was funny though. There was a White House hairdresser and everything, but unless they were going somewhere really important, her mother usually cut Neal's hair because they both got a kick out of it. Quality time.

"I have to go eat," he said.

"Have a nice time."

"Will you play pool with me?" he asked, not quite looking at her since she had always made it pretty vocally obvious that she hated pool.

She grinned. "Not a chance, pal."

CHAPTER NINETEEN

That night, Trudy came into her room.

"Am I interrupting anything?" she asked, carrying her crocheting. She was making a coat for Kirby.

"No," Meg said, pushing her French—*plus-que-par-fait* exercises—away.

Trudy sat in the old rocking chair, settling herself comfortably. She put on her glasses and squinted at the yarn in her bag. "Time to add some green?"

"Yeah," Meg said. "He looks good in green."

Trudy nodded, taking out her crochet hook. Then, she fumbled in the pocket of her cardigan, pulling out, with a big smile, what was left of a package of gumdrops. "Look what I have."

"Can I have some?"

"I think that could be arranged." Trudy leaned over to hand her the package and Meg helped herself to a licorice one, two yellows and an orange, then gave the package back, Trudy selecting a pink one. "When you three were little," Trudy said, "all I had to do to make you happy was give you a gumdrop and maybe hold you in my lap for a minute."

"And Vick's Vaporub," Meg said.

Trudy nodded. "For nightmares."

Meg thought back, remembering many nights of waking up crying and having Trudy be the one to come because her mother was in Washington. Trudy or her father.

"I feel very lucky," Trudy said. "Being blessed with *two* wonderful families. A lot of people don't even have one."

Meg nodded.

"I'm going back to Florida in a couple of days."

"To be with your son?" Meg asked.

"That too," Trudy said. "I also think it's time for all of you to be alone. I'm starting to be in the way."

"But—I mean, you could never—"

"I just think it's time," Trudy said. "You need to work things out together."

"We need *you.*"

"You need me to go away," Trudy said.

"But—"

"I'll be back before Christmas." She smiled a very loving smile. "Would I neglect my grandchildren?"

Meg tried to smile back, but swallowed instead, afraid that she was going to cry.

"You'll be all right," Trudy said. "I have great faith in you."

"It's hard," Meg said.

"It always is." She picked up her crochet hook, starting a green row. "But, don't worry. You can do it."

Meg watched the row get longer, seeming to grow magically. "Trudy?"

Trudy glanced up.

"Can I have another gumdrop?"

On Wednesday, Josh had jazz band practice and Meg decided to stay after and wait for him.

"You going to come watch me?" he asked.

She shook her head. "I'll distract you."

"No, you won't. It'll make me play better."

"It'll make you show off."

He grinned. "Probably."

"Look, I'll just hang out in the library. Come get me when you're finished."

"Are you sure?"

She nodded. "I'll get some work done. I'm still kind of behind."

In spite of good intentions, once she was in the library, she wasn't really in the mood for homework. She glanced at the clock—jazz band would probably run for an hour.

She stood up, wandering in the direction of the fiction

section, but ending up in the political science section instead. It was sort of on the meager side, but, since this was Washington, probably better than most school libraries.

There were a lot of Kennedy books. Books about assassinations. Martin Luther King, Anwar Sadat—probably even books about John Lennon. It was always the likable ones—Kennedy, Jerry Ford—her mother. Popular Presidents were much more likely to be targets. There had to be some kind of lesson there, but whatever it was, Meg didn't like it.

She took down a book she had read before, a scary book called *Four Days*. November 22, 1963 through November 25, 1963. Over twenty years ago. She hadn't even been alive then, and it was still a part of her life. Of every American's life.

The book was full of photographs: the window where Lee Harvey Oswald had been waiting, Kennedy actually being shot, Jack Ruby shooting Oswald, the funeral—horrible pictures. The worst of all was the famous shot of Jackie Kennedy leaving the plane, her dress bloodstained.

Meg shuddered, closing the book. The day it happened, when she finally saw her father, he had been wearing a different outfit. The old one must have been—Jesus. She shivered, feeling very cold.

"Meg?"

She looked up to see her English teacher, Mrs. Hayes. "Oh, um," she stood up to be polite, "hello."

"I saw you from up there," Mrs. Hayes indicated the checkout desk, where Meg could see a stack of books, "and I wanted to be sure you were all right."

"Yes. Thank you."

Mrs. Hayes glanced at the Kennedy book. "You should stay away from things like that."

"Yes, ma'am. I should." Meg looked at her in her casual wool skirt and light blue sweater, highlighted by a single silver chain, wondering what it would be like to have a mother who was an English teacher. A mother who sometimes overslept, a mother who got angry when people didn't pitch in around the house, a mother who would run down to the store in old jeans and a sweatshirt. A normal mother.

Mrs. Hayes carried the book back to the political science section and Meg thought about mothers who were in the house, mothers who worked in banks, mothers who were doctors and nurses.

"I recommend Anne Tyler," her teacher said with a smile, having replaced the book.

"Yes, ma'am. I've read a couple," Meg said, wondering how many children Mrs. Hayes had. Did she have to cook dinner when she got home from school, or did her husband do it? Looking at her, Meg had the feeling that she was going to go home and cook spaghetti and meatballs.

"I hope you'll feel well enough to come back to the newspaper soon. We miss you."

Meg flushed. She had sort of been neglecting extracurricular activities lately. "Yeah. Next week maybe?"

"Whenever you feel ready."

"Thank you." Meg shifted her weight, starting to feel embarrassed. She had never been one to talk to teachers much.

Mrs. Hayes smiled and patted her on the shoulder, very normal-motherish.

"C-can I ask you a stupid question?" Meg put her hands in her pockets, then took them out. "I mean, may I?"

Mrs. Hayes nodded, her expression amused.

"Do you live in a house?"

Her teacher looked startled.

"I mean, as opposed to an apartment or Crystal City or whatever."

Her teacher smiled. "Yes, I live in a house."

"Where—" Meg smiled back shyly. "I don't know. Where you have to rake leaves and everything? And carry the trash cans down to the driveway? And a little twerpy kid delivers the papers?"

Mrs. Hayes laughed. "My son."

"Oh," Meg said, embarrassed. "I'm sorry. I didn't mean to—"

"I know. Did you live in a neighborhood like that in Massachusetts?"

"Yeah," Meg said, remembering it. "I mean, pretty much. I mean, Mom was the Senator and stuff, but it was still like that. Trick-or-treating and Christmas caroling and all of that."

Mrs. Hayes nodded. "You have a very close family, don't you?"

Meg thought about that. "Yeah. We do. I mean, lots of times, we fight and stuff, but—" She looked at her teacher uncertainly. "That's normal, isn't it?"

"Very normal."

Meg looked at the clock. "I bet you have to go pick someone up from ballet."

Her teacher also checked the clock. "Soccer," she said.

Soccer. Her brothers had always played soccer. That is, until Steven got on this basketball kick. When Mrs. Hayes was gone, she sat back down, thinking about Massachusetts. Like about the garden they had had. Sort of an ugly garden, in Meg's opinion, but her father was really into the idea. On weekends sometimes, he would make the whole family go out and work in it. He always ran the show, drinking Molson and wearing sweatshirts without any sleeves. Pretty macho stuff. Her mother would put on a bandanna, sip iced tea, and talk about "cultivating the rich brown earth," although mostly she would just stand around. Her mother was what you would call a city slicker. Meg and Steven would always get in trouble for spraying the hose around and Neal would get yelled at for weeding biennials. They weren't exactly peaceful afternoons, but still. In spite of making constant disparaging comments, Meg had always enjoyed them.

"Hey," Josh said.

"Oh, hi." She stood up, putting her knapsack on her shoulder. "How was band?"

"Pretty good," he said, bouncing a little, which meant that he still had a rhythm in his head. "Get any work done?"

"Lots."

172

They walked out of the library, Josh still bouncing. Kind of annoying, but also endearing.

"Hey." She put her arm around his shoulders. "Buy you an ice cream, sailor?"

He stopped bouncing. "I'm still waiting to collect on that drink."

"I'll buy you ice cream instead."

"Are you allowed? I mean," he gestured over his shoulder towards her agents, "don't you have to ask them?"

Meg scowled. Nothing like having two authoritative little shadows. "You ask them, okay?"

"Meg—"

"Please?"

He sighed, but nodded, going back to ask.

They ended up in Baskin-Robbins, with sundaes. People recognized her in the store—the Secret Service cars outside didn't help—but Josh had a baseball cap in his gym bag and she put it on, which made things a little better. Even the slightest disguise worked to discourage people. Lots of times, although she felt like a jerk, she would wear sunglasses. Her parents always suggested hats, and Preston had given her a Catholic University sweatshirt, which seemed to work the best of all.

"Pretty quiet," Josh said.

"Yeah, I know. I'm sorry."

"You're still not speaking to your agents?"

"They bug me," she said.

He nodded, obviously refraining from comment.

"I'm sorry," she said. "We're supposed to be having a good time."

He shrugged. "We can go eat these in the car."

She shook her head, not in the mood to sit in the backseat with her agents in the front. "Here's better."

"Whatever." He looked around. "They're probably just staring at you because you're so beautiful."

She relaxed. "I'm not beautiful."

"Oh, yeah?" He started to stand. "You want me to ask them?"

"No!" She grabbed his sweater to pull him down. "Don't be a jerk."

He pretended to be crushed. "You think I'm a jerk?"

"Yes."

They sat holding hands, Josh looking so interested in the half a sundae she had left that she gave it to him.

"I was looking at a book about Kennedy in the library," she said.

He stopped eating. "Not so bright."

"Not really," she agreed. She picked up her cup of water, swallowing some. "I guess things could be a lot worse."

"Things could *always* be worse," he said.

"You think so?"

"Sure. I always figure you should be happy with the problems you have."

"*Happy?*"

"Happy that they're not any worse."

Meg frowned. "I can't tell if that's optimistic or not."

"What, you never read *Candide*?"

"I read *Candide*," she said, offended.

"Okay then." He picked up his spoon. "Consider yourself lucky."

"Lucky." She watched him eat, imagining worse scenarios. The bullet two inches to the right, or hitting her in the spine, or—or hitting her father too, or—she shuddered. Enough of imagining worse scenarios.

"Things could be worse," he said.

"That's for sure." She looked at his hand in hers, feeling the bones and piano-strengthened tendons. "Could I ask you something personal?"

His grin was rakish. "Go for it."

"What's the worst thing that ever happened to you?"

"Other than you not speaking to me for a week?"

She nodded, very serious.

"Oh." The grin left. "I don't know. The, uh, the divorce was pretty bad."

She nodded, expecting that.

"And, uh," his hand tightened, "when my, uh, my mother had the mastectomy."

Meg glanced away from his hand, startled. "She did? You never—I mean—"

"Tenth grade," he said and she could hear him swallow. "It was pretty bad."

"I'm sorry." She also swallowed. "Is she—okay now?"

"Far as we know," he said, his voice stiff.

"I'm really sorry." She lifted his hand to hold it to her lips for a second. "How come you never told me about it?"

"I don't like to think about it."

"I'm sorry."

"Well." He straightened his glasses. "At this point, we just go through a few bad days every six months when she goes in for her checkup."

"And you never mentioned it?"

He shrugged. "It just would have made you paranoid about *your* mother."

"No, it—" She stopped. Of course it would have. Incredibly paranoid.

"I don't mean that in a bad way," he said. "I just—well, even before all of this, you were pretty hung up. I mean, about something happening to her."

"I always have been," Meg said quietly.

"Well, yeah," he nodded. "I know. Because of her not being around much and all."

"I feel like a jerk."

"It's not like I haven't had to pry things out of *you*."

"What," she had to grin, "I'm not candid?"

He laughed. "No, you're not candid."

"I'm trying," she said. "With you, I mean."

"I know." He smiled. "So am I."

She nodded, and they held hands more tightly.

"Things aren't supposed to happen to parents," she said.

"Yeah," he agreed. "It's a lot scarier when it's parents."

They didn't speak, Meg thinking about her mother at home in the White House, trying to get better, Josh presumably thinking about his.

"Well," he said. "Enough of this banter. Can I buy you a Tab, scullery maid?"

"*Scullery maid?*"

"Can I buy you a Tab, wench?"

She grinned. "Go for it, sailor."

CHAPTER TWENTY

"Well, this is good," Beth said on the phone that night. "This is all very good. I like your checking in like this."

Meg laughed. "I suppose I can expect a bill for your services."

"Well, yes," Beth said. "I've decided that a terribly garish and expensive Christmas present isn't enough."

"Yeah, well, garish you can count on. Don't hold your breath on expensive."

"After all these years, I've grown to expect that," Beth said sadly. "Hey, speaking of presents, your mother's really funny—she sent me a thank-you note for the book and everything."

"She really liked it. I heard her laughing when she was reading it even."

"Well, it's a funny book," Beth said. "Over *your* head, of course, but—"

"I read it," Meg said. "I got a couple of the jokes."

"I know, dear. You do try hard."

"Just can't quite measure up, right?"

"No," Beth said, sounding regretful now. "I'm sorry."

"Eats you up inside, right?"

"Yes, very much so." Her voice changed back to normal. "Hey, want to hear the Scoop of the Month? You'll never guess who asked me out."

"Oh—Rick Hamilton," Meg guessed. From fourth grade on, when Rick had moved to Chestnut Hill, just about every girl in the grade had had a crush on him. La crème de la crème.

"Yeah, actually," Beth said, sounding slightly disappointed that she had guessed.

"My God, really? He's never gone out with anyone who has brown hair before."

"I know." Beth sighed extra deeply. "I guess it's my lot in life to be successful."

"Oh, yeah. Absolutely."

Beth laughed. "Well—maybe. What do you think I should wear?"

"A hat," Meg said. "Definitely a hat."

Although Meg had a lot of makeup work to do in the next few days, she did manage to make time to watch "Hill Street Blues" with Josh on Thursday, play tennis on the White House court with Alison after school on Friday, and go to a movie with everyone on Saturday night. Getting back into the social scene definitely made things easier.

Late Sunday afternoon, as she worked on calculus, her mother came into her room, walking slowly. She looked very tired, and because she wasn't being the President, was hunched over her side, favoring her injuries.

"My goodness," she said. "I thought *I* was a workaholic."

Meg glanced up at her, feeling cross-eyed. Let s equals $f(t)$ be the position versus time curve for a particle moving in the positive direction along—

"Why don't you take a break?" her mother suggested.

—a coordinate line. Solve for— "I have to finish," Meg said.

"Take a break," her mother said, more firmly.

Bow to the authority figure. Meg put her pen down. Relative extremum be damned.

"What are you doing?" her mother wanted to know.

Meg shook her head. "Don't ask."

Her mother moved the rocking chair a little closer to the window and sat down. "One thing I'd suggest."

"What's that?"

"When you're doing a lot of close work, you should look up every twenty minutes or so and focus on something far away. Exercise your eyes a bit. That way, you won't tire as quickly.''

Presidential advice. Hmmm. Meg got up to focus out the window.

"See anything interesting?" her mother asked.

"Lafayette Park."

Her mother nodded, rocking in the chair.

"Gets dark early these days," Meg said.

"Winter," her mother agreed.

Meg listened to the rockers against the carpet, a sad little sound. What an odd sight they must be: Meg standing by the window, staring out at the darkening city, her mother rocking. The President and the First Daughter audition for a Bergman movie.

"Quiet without Trudy," her mother said.

"Yeah."

"She'll be back at Christmas though."

Meg nodded.

"What do you think about Camp David for Thanksgiving?"

"Will you be well enough?"

"Yes," her mother said, her voice determined. "We need to go away from here for a while."

Meg nodded.

"No reporters, no one cooking for us—with luck, no anything."

"Are we allowed?" Meg asked uncertainly.

Her mother laughed. "I'm going to be *very* assertive."

Meg thought about Camp David, about how nice and quiet and peaceful it was. Trees and grass and lots of hiking trails and stuff. Of course, it would be a major production—Secret Service all over the place, Dr. Brooks and other medical people, aides galore—but even so. "Sounds really good," she said.

"I think so too."

"Uh, Mom?" Steven said, at the door.

She smiled at him. "What?"

"Dad wants to know if you want to have dinner now, or wait, or what."

She looked at Meg. "What do you think?"

"I'm kind of hungry." Meg said.

"Well then, my goodness." Her mother stood, surreptitiously cautious with her side. "Let's go."

"Are we having anything queer and soft tonight?" Steven asked.

"Well, I don't know," their mother said. "We've certainly been eating our share of soft food lately, haven't we?" She put her arm around him. "I *did* request that we be given some nice hard rocks and minerals this evening, but we'll have to see what happens."

"Nuts and bolts," Meg contributed.

Steven grinned and moved closer to their mother, allowing himself to be somewhat less cool than usual. "How come everyone's in like, such a good mood?"

"Oh, I don't know." Their mother straightened his collar, tucking it into his sweater. "Because we're happy to see you."

"No way," he said, but looked very pleased.

Meg smiled at no one and nothing in particular—well, Vanessa, maybe—feeling an unexpected goodness in the air as she followed them down to the West Sitting Hall, where Neal was on her father's lap, watching him read the Book Reviews. Meg's father looked worried, seeing how slowly her mother was walking, but she winked at him and his expression relaxed.

The good feeling continued through dinner, everyone careful not to destroy it, although Steven made cracks about the macaroni and cheese which was, indeed, pretty soft food. After dinner, they went to the Presidential Bedroom to watch a tape of one of her mother's favorite movies, *Bringing Up Baby*. Katharine Hepburn, Cary Grant, hysterically funny. Felix brought popcorn in.

Meg hung out after the movie to watch the news with her parents. It was sort of silly to watch the news with the President of the United States. Especially during stories when a small grin would spread across her mother's face and Meg would know that there was more to it than was being reported.

She cheerfully ate popcorn and drank Tab while her mother skimmed papers and her father read. Then, a story came on about Sampson, the would-be assassin, because the hospital was about to release a psychiatric evaluation, probably the next day. Meg gulped her mouthful of Tab, almost choking, and her parents stopped talking. The story was mostly speculative, although it included a clip from an interview with the psychiatrist who had examined him early on and declared him insane—psychotic with possible schizophrenia, manifesting itself in violent criminal— Meg closed her eyes, trying not to listen. Why had they watched the stupid news? Should she change the channel? Or just wait for it to end, or—the anchorperson switched to a different story and Meg held her breath, afraid to look at her parents and see their reactions. She glanced over swiftly and saw her father looking at her mother, who was looking at her arm and the sling.

"Well," her mother spoke quietly, "I hope he gets help."

School went well on Monday. In fact, she knew things were better because she was having a terrible time paying attention, but now it was for normal reasons. Like because it was more fun to draw pictures of Vanessa or pass notes to people or stare at Josh. She loved to stare at him when he didn't know she was doing it. Like in French. French was his favorite subject, so he usually paid attention and volunteered answers and everything. She could watch him all period long and he wouldn't even notice. Sometimes Mr. Thénardier did, but Josh almost never did.

He was cute to watch. He would frown when he was listening and adjust his glasses about every five seconds. He also drummed his pen in quiet staccato rhythms. It kind of made her wonder what unconscious idiotic habits *she* had, other than the fact that lots of times she pretended that she had ski boots on, which completely changed the way she walked and stood. No one ever commented on it. One didn't question the President's daughter's motor co-ordination.

So what with staring and passing notes and drawing Vanessa, the day passed pretty pleasantly. They had a great time in Current Issues because Alison was selling M&M's for the choir, and they spent most of the period throwing them at various targets around the room whenever Mr. Murphy turned his back. Meg's hand slipped with an orange M&M and she bounced it off Mr. Murphy's file cabinet instead of the Smokey the Bear poster. Mr. Murphy was not amused. Meg and her friends were. He threatened that if he caught anyone, they would stay after school and spend an hour crawling around on their hands and knees, picking up scraps of paper and other improperly discarded trash. Sounded like a fun time.

"The pencil sharpener," Nathan whispered when Mr. Murphy was at the board again and they threw yellow M&M's, all of which missed, clattering on the floor. Mr. Murphy decided to stop writing on the board and gave his "this is a class of seniors and I don't expect this sort of infantile behavior" speech. They were infantile enough to laugh.

After school, Meg drifted to Student Council, the first meeting she'd attended since the shooting. The advisor just smiled and said, "Good to have you back," and she ended up being in charge of decorations for the Christmas Dance. Snowflake city. When the meeting was over, she wandered outside with Alison and Zachary and everyone, her agents—she still had double protection—behind her.

Nathan grinned at her. "You into it, Powers?"

She grinned back. "Into what?"

"Woody Allen festival. Friday night. Be there."

"Yeah, really? Downtown?"

He nodded.

"Well, yeah. Sounds great."

Everyone said good-bye, meandering off towards cars and public transportation, and Meg stood on the sidewalk with Josh.

"I'll call you after my lesson," he said.

She nodded and he leaned over to give her a chaste kiss.

"After dinner too," he said.

"Okay." She watched him run to get into Zachary's car, then turned to go to her own, agents closer now. The wind was cold and she hunched down into her sweater. Winter was definitely coming. She waved as Zachary and Josh drove by, Zachary beeping his horn, then put her hand back in her pocket, out of the wind.

They were about ten feet away from the car when there was a loud bang from somewhere, kind of like a gun or a firecracker, and before Meg had a chance to react, she found herself on the sidewalk. One of her agents was on top of her, shielding her with his body, while the other crouched above them in shooting position, his body a wide target, facing the direction from which the sound had come, his gun out and leveled. She heard the other two agents run over, also in front of her.

"Is it a car?" Wayne shouted, on top of her. "I think it was a car!"

After some tense seconds, a minute maybe, Gary and the other two agents established that it had indeed been a car backfiring, and Wayne lifted Meg up, brushing her off and hustling her to the car, another agent on her other side.

"You okay?" Wayne asked, out of breath, as Gary jumped into the front seat.

"Y-yeah," Meg said, trembling. "I mean—" She fluttered her hand across her face. "I'm fine."

"Chuck, get her knapsack!" Wayne said through the window at the fourth agent, and then the car was speeding away, all kinds of people staring after them. Meg closed her eyes and leaned back, not wanting anyone to know how scared she had been.

"I'm sorry," Wayne was saying. "We're—overcautious lately."

She nodded, the inside of her head jangling.

"I'm sorry." He dabbed her cheek with his handkerchief. "You've got a scrape there."

Meg opened her eyes, feeling dazed, aware that her cheek was stinging.

"Let me see your hands," he said, trying to open her right fist.

With an effort, she unclenched them and saw that they were gravel-scraped and bleeding slightly, like when she was six and used to fall off her bike all the time.

He frowned. "Sorry about that. We'll get you right down to Brooks and have him fix you up."

"I'm fine," Meg said, which was a lie. She took a few deep breaths, still shaking, her nerves so jarred that it was hard not to cry. She rested her face in her hands, listening to Dennis, the agent in the passenger's seat, call the incident in.

"Thank you," she said weakly.

They all nodded, and she could tell that they were almost as scared as she was. She put her face back in her hands, trying to calm down. If that had been a gun and the person had had good aim, she might be—she closed her eyes more tightly.

When they pulled up at the South Portico, she stayed in the car for a minute, wanting to recover herself before getting out in front of the reporters who had gathered.

With an effort, she sat up, looking at her agents. "Y-you guys didn't have to do that."

Wayne's expression stiffened. "I'm sorry. We overreacted."

Meg shook her head. "I meant, protect me. I've been so—I mean, lately—I mean, you didn't have to—"

"Come on." Wayne put his hand on her back, helping her out of the car. "Let's take you inside."

"Yeah, but—"

"Just come on."

Dr. Brooks was waiting inside and she was rushed right into his office to have the scrapes cleaned and bandaged. As he waited for the antiseptic to dry, he lifted her wrist to check her pulse. "Pretty scary stuff," he remarked, unwrapping a roll of gauze.

Meg was going to be cool and cavalier, but since she was still trembling, didn't bother. "Yeah."

He patted her knee. "Any of these new?" He indicated the rips.

"Um, that one." She pointed to a tear below her right knee and he separated the cloth to check.

"Uh-hunh," he nodded. "You've got another one there."

She protested against all of the gauze, but no one ever took chances with the First Family.

"You're sure you're okay," he said.

She nodded. "Thank you." She looked at her hands, clumsy with the gauze. When she was little, no one ever gave her gauze. She would run into the house crying, Trudy would wash her off, make her laugh and send her back out again.

Her father hurried in, looking very worried, and when Meg saw him, she had to grip the sides of her chair to keep herself from crying. He bent to hug her, and then she *knew* she was going to cry.

"Okay," he said gently. "Don't worry, it's okay."

"Just a few scrapes, Russell," Dr. Brooks said. "She's more shaken up than anything else."

Meg kept her face hidden, embarrassed. "Is it okay if we go upstairs?"

Her father nodded and she was able to keep the tears back until they were getting off the elevator, and he led her across the hall to the Presidential Bedroom, sitting her down on the couch.

"It's okay." He hugged her. "Go ahead."

"They were really fast," she said weakly. "Knocking me down."

He nodded.

"I thought it was—I mean, it could have been—" She gulped a deep breath, unexpectedly close to falling apart.

"Go ahead. You'll feel better."

Meg shook her head, her fists tight. "I shouldn't," she said, gulping. "I shouldn't be upset because something *could* have happened when Mom—I mean, nothing happened, I shouldn't—"

"I think you should," her father said. "To my knowledge, you haven't yet."

"But—" She tried to stop the tears and they came harder. "I mean—"

"Shh. Don't try to stop."

"But Steven and Neal don't—"

"At least one of them has come to our room every night."

She gulped. "Really?"

He nodded.

"What about you? Have you—?"

"Yes," he said. "More than once."

She looked at him, tears running down her cheeks.

"It's good for you," he said. "You invariably feel better afterwards."

"But—"

"Relax," he said.

His arm was comforting on her shoulders, and she cried until she was too tired to keep going, except for an occasional weak gulp.

"Better?" he asked.

"I guess so." She wiped her sleeve slowly across her eyes, a few stray tears still coming out. "I don't understand why he would hurt her."

"It's the position, Meg. Not the person."

"What about her being a woman?"

"I don't know," he said. "Maybe he hates his mother, or his girlfriend, or someone. Maybe he just hates seeing a woman achieve so much. There are a lot of people like that."

"It's not fair."

"No, it isn't." He sighed. "I don't know what to tell you, Meg."

"She has three more years."

He nodded.

"Well, what if—" She stopped guiltily.

"You can't spend the whole three years worrying about it. I mean," he frowned, "I think that would be equally destructive."

"So you think everything's going to be okay?" She looked up at him, feeling like Neal.

"Insofar as things can be controlled."

"That's not very far."

"Well, I don't know," he said. "The Secret Service does a damn good job. People only hear about it on the few occasions that they *can't* prevent something."

"You mean, things have *almost* happened?"

Her father hesitated.

"Like if Mom's going to speak somewhere," Meg said, already knowing the answer, "and they switch locations. They must do that for a reason."

Her father nodded reluctantly. "She gets a lot of threats, Meg. Unfortunately, it comes with the job."

"Have there been—attempts?"

"Foiled ones, yes," he said.

"L-like what?"

"Does it matter?"

"Yes."

He sighed. "I don't know. A man on a roof in Chicago. Someone carrying a homemade bomb in Philadelphia."

"How come I didn't know about them?"

"Your mother hasn't even known about them until after. The Secret Service does a very good, quiet job."

"Then how come—I mean—"

"They can't always prevent things," he said quietly. "No one could."

She slouched down. "I've been really mean to them lately. Not speaking to them or anything."

"I imagine you feel differently now."

She nodded, flushing.

"Don't worry. They understand how you've been feeling."

"I hope so." She looked at her gauze-wrapped hands. "Can I redo the *Seventeen* thing?"

He nodded. "I think that would be a good idea. I'll talk to Preston."

They sat silently for a minute.

"Dad? Can I ask you something?"

"You may," he said. Her parents were heavily into correcting their children's grammar.

"If you were in a room with him, and you had a gun, would you hurt him?"

He didn't answer right away.

"Like remember when she broke her leg? And you like, tried to take that guy apart?"

"I tried to slug him," her father said defensively. "Not take him apart."

"Yeah, but all he did was ski in front of her. This is a lot worse."

He nodded.

"Would you hurt him?"

"It wouldn't really solve anything," he said, then smiled slightly. "That's not to say that I wouldn't mind punching him pretty hard."

"I wouldn't mind punching him myself," Meg said.

"I don't suppose any of us would." His smile was very wry and almost a grin. "However."

"Yeah." Meg looked at her gauze. "Can I take this junk off? I mean, it's only a couple of scrapes."

He glanced around, at this place called the White House, and this time, he did grin. "Sure. Just put on a Band-Aid if you need one."

CHAPTER TWENTY-ONE

She had barely gotten to her bedroom when her phone rang.

She picked it up. "Hello?"

"Hey, kid," Preston said, sounding amused. "I just got a call from the South Gate—seems your friend Josh is practically breaking it down, trying to get in here. You want me to have him sent up?"

Meg smiled. "Yeah." She went downstairs, stepping outside just as Josh drove up in an unfamiliar car.

He jumped out, looking very upset. "My God, you *are* hurt!"

"I'm fine," she said. "It's just a couple of scrapes."

"What happened? Jimmy Tucker called and said he saw your agents knock you down, then drive away about a hundred miles an hour—" he didn't wait for an answer— "My God, your poor face! Are you all right? What happened?"

"I'm fine." She put her hands on his shoulders, seeing that he was literally shaking with worry. "A car backfired, that's all. Don't worry."

"Don't *worry?* Meg, you might have been—I mean, I thought—"

"I'm fine. Come on," she sat him down on the steps, "it's okay. Really."

"Jesus Christ," he said weakly. "I thought—I mean, I about had a heart attack." Shakily, he wiped his sleeve across his face. "I really thought—" He shook his head. "Are you *sure* you're all right?"

"Yes." She put her arms around him, feeling his heart pound against her chest as he hung on to her. "Shh," she said softly. "It's okay."

They kept hugging, Meg feeling his heartbeat and breathing slow down.

"Okay?" she asked, her mouth next to his ear.

He nodded, turning his face to kiss her, a long kiss that left both of them out of breath.

"Whose car is that?" she asked.

He grinned sheepishly. "My piano teacher's. I guess I kind of freaked."

"And he trusted you to drive?"

"If he hadn't, I swear to God I would have smacked him."

Meg laughed. "You and my father."

"Your father wants to smack my piano teacher?"

Meg laughed again. "No, he—" She stopped, seeing his grin. "You jerk." She leaned forward to hug him some more. "Can you come upstairs, or do you have to get the car back?"

"I don't know. I mean, I should probably—I'd rather come upstairs."

"Look, take the car back before *he* has a heart attack."

"Yeah." He sighed. "I guess." He looked at her, eyes worried again. "Are you *sure* you're all right? I mean, all those bandages—"

"You know how they are around here."

"Yeah." He kissed each of her hands, her cheek, and then her mouth, staying at her mouth the longest. "I'm going to call you, okay? More than once, probably."

Meg smiled, hugging him tightly. "It's okay with me."

She got several other phone calls, including one from Beth, after the early news, most stations apparently mentioning the incident, even though there wasn't any film footage. Meg assured everyone that she was fine—just a couple of scrapes, no big deal. But getting the phone calls felt nice.

Her mother didn't hear about it until she came upstairs for dinner and she was very concerned. This spread to Steven and Neal, who bent over backwards being kind to her. Steven even held her chair at dinner. Meg felt like a fool and escaped to her room shortly after the meal to write college essays. In theory.

She picked up *A Moveable Feast*, pushing Vanessa off her pillow so she could lie down. It was a book by Ernest Hemingway about his days in Paris, hanging out with Gertrude Stein and F. Scott Fitzgerald, and at a really famous bookstore called Shakespeare and Company. It must have been kind of fun to be a lost generation. Maybe someday she and Beth should spend time being officially disaffected.

After a while, Neal showed up, holding a mug of cocoa.

"Meggie?" he asked, behind her threshold.

"Don't be a jerk," she said. "You know you can come in."

He carried the mug over to her, smiling and putting it on her night table. "It's to help you work on your essays."

Meg flushed. "I was just sort of *reading* essays first," she said, pointing to her book. "Like to warm up."

He nodded, believing her.

"Thanks for the cocoa. Aren't you going to have some too?"

He smiled and she noticed the chocolate mustache. "We did."

"Oh. I see."

He stood there, smiling at her, and he was so cute that she smiled back.

"I have to go to bed now," he said.

"It's getting late," she agreed.

"Will you play pool tomorrow?"

She laughed. "Sure."

He climbed onto the bed to hug her. "I'm glad you aren't hurt," he said, his voice muffled against her shoulder.

"Me too." She ruffled up his hair, which was freshly trimmed. "I like you even though you're an ugly peasant."

He giggled. "I'm not ugly."

"Yeah, but you're a peasant."

He giggled again. "You're the ugly Queen."

"I'm the *beautiful* Queen."

"Blech," he said.

"Come on." She started to lift him up, but he was too heavy. "You're a *fat* peasant."

"I'm not fat."

"Well, you're getting big then."

"Where are we going?" he asked.

"To get me some Oreos so I can work, and you some Oreos so you can sleep."

When she had some Oreos, and her father had taken Neal in to bed, she went to see what Steven was doing, finding him on his bed, reading. Definitely a member of her family.

"You busy?" she asked.

He didn't look up. "Don't you knock?"

"No. How are you?"

He shrugged.

"I thought I'd say good night."

He nodded. "Good night."

"I also thought I'd sit in here for a while."

"I kind of want to be alone," he said.

"Want a cookie?"

He glanced over and took two from her hand, leaving her with one.

"That was singular," she said.

He stopped chewing. "You want it back?"

"No, thanks." She sat on the bottom of his bed. "Today was kind of scary."

"Kind of?" he asked.

"Remember when Trevor died?" Trevor was the German Shepherd they had had before Kirby. "You know how it was really bad at first, and then, it was only bad sometimes? Like if you remembered it all of a sudden, and you would feel like crying all over again?"

"I *still* remember it sometimes," he said.

"Well, yeah, me too. I guess we always will."

"What, and this is going to be like that?"

192

"It makes sense, doesn't it?"

"Swell," he said.

"Swell?" she asked. "What is this, 1950?"

"You always say it."

"That's different. *I* am the Queen."

"Oh, Christ," he said. "Not that again."

"You're just jealous."

He took her last Oreo. "If you say so." He stopped when the cookie was already in his mouth. "Did you want this or anything?" he asked, his mouth full.

"Not now that it has peasant germs."

He grinned. "You only *wish* you had some of my germs."

"Every time I see the first star," she said, nodding.

"Bet you wish on your birthday too."

"Every year," she nodded. She punched him lightly on the shoulder and stood up to go work on her essays.

"You look fine," he said.

"Fine?" she asked, confused.

"Your face." He gestured to his own cheek. "In case you thought you looked ugly or something."

"Oh." Self-consciously, she touched the scrape. "Thank you."

He shrugged. "Wasn't lying or anything."

"Thank you. I'm flattered."

He shrugged and picked up his book.

"See you in the morning," she said.

"Yup," he said.

She went back to her room where her cocoa was quite cold. She carried it and Vanessa over to her desk, setting them down and taking a stack of college applications out of her top drawer.

The question was, where to start. The essays were a major pain. Admissions offices probably got sick of reading about other people's significant experiences. It was even more boring to *write* about them. She sighed and took out a legal pad, picking up her pen.

"I have had a lot of significant experiences. This makes

193

it very difficult to choose one." Oh, yeah, real original. A grabber. Try again.

"On Monday, January 21 of this year, my mother was sworn in as the President of the United States." Just in case they hadn't noticed that 1600 Pennsylvania Avenue was her home address.

Page three. *"Call me Meghan."* Yeah, right. Give it up, kid.

Page four. *"If you really want to hear about it, the first thing you'll probably want to know is where I was born, and what my lousy childhood was like, and—"* Very original. With just a little help from J. D. Salinger.

Page five. This sure was wasting a lot of paper. Maybe she should just give up and try some other time. *"To be honest,"* she wrote, *"I don't know if I really want to go to college. It just kind of seems like the thing to do."* Then, why are you applying, dear? Next application, please.

At this rate, she wasn't going to be conserving too many trees tonight. She turned and looked at the telephone next to her bed. Maybe she should call Josh and talk to him. Again.

"Nothing significant has ever happened to me," she wrote. *"I lead a very dull life and can't imagine why any college anywhere would want me or even if I want them—"* Garbage, garbage, garbage.

She slouched down in her chair, lifting Vanessa onto her lap. *"You want to do this for me? I'll give you speech-writer rate."*

Vanessa kneaded her paws in Meg's sweater.

"This is a major drag," Meg said. "I'm really not into this."

Vanessa purred.

One more try. *"The thing about most of my significant experiences is that they happened to my mother. I've never run for President. I've never been a world leader. I've never walked into gunfire. But even though I've never done any of those things, they've affected me."* She paused. Maybe this wasn't such a great idea. *"In my family, small things end up being so large-scale that you kind of feel like stepping out and observing them, not participating. Not experiencing. Like this picture I saw recently.''* She hesitated. Heading for dangerous territory there. Oh, well. Damn the torpedoes. *''There was a girl sitting on a bench with her head in her hands and you could tell that she was trying as hard as she could not to fall apart. And the caption said, The First Daughter, in a moment of private grief. And I looked at it, and all I could think was that it belonged in some Year-in-Review issue. I mean, it was a really disturbing, thought-provoking picture, a horrible moment, caught on film. Except it was me.''*

Meg lowered her pen, skimming what she had written so far. Sentimental tripe. Emotionally manipulating. But accurate. She walked over to her dresser, pulling that particular magazine out of the drawer where she had hidden it, underneath her nightgowns. She looked at the First Daughter's private grief. What you might call pretty public privacy. She looked at the gray Levi's and the shoulders hunched into the Fair Isle sweater, then closed the magazine, returning to her desk.

''When I came home that night, there was chicken soup. Very yellow, with big chunks of chicken and thick noodles. I think Carl makes the pasta himself. There were also grilled cheese sandwiches, with Neal's crusts cut off to make him happy, but my stomach hurt and I went down to my room to pat my cat. I patted her most of the night. There was a 'Love Boat' rerun on, and Steven talked me into watching it with him. We did, but I don't remember who the guest stars were or anything. I do remember a McDonald's commercial being on because it was one we liked, but neither of us laughed. I guess it didn't seem very funny. Under the circumstances. So I looked out the window at the Washington Monument. All bright and lit up and brave-looking. When we were still living in Massachusetts, I remember someone once threatened to dynamite the monument and a SWAT team blew him away instead. You really have to wonder. Not that I know the answer. It seems like there might not be one. I don't know.''

She stopped writing. Could she write "I don't know" in a college essay? Was any of this like a college essay? Maybe you weren't allowed.

"Working hard?" her mother said.

"What?" Meg turned to see her just inside the door, a bathrobe draped over her shoulders, covering the sling. "Yeah, kind of."

"Are you getting much accomplished?"

"Probably not." Meg turned the legal pad over, too embarrassed to have her mother read it.

"Is there anything I can help you with?"

"No, thanks." Meg leaned forward, weight on her right foot, pretending she had on a ski boot.

"Are you sure you're all right?"

Meg stopped leaning on her foot. "Yeah, I was just—oh." Her mother probably hadn't even noticed the ski boot. "I mean, yeah."

Her mother bent to examine her scrape, then straightened, apparently satisfied. "As long as you're sure."

"I'm fine." Meg looked at her mother, who was only slightly hunched now and less so every day. And it had been quite a while since Meg had seen her face tighten in pain. "Are *you* better?"

Her mother nodded. "Much."

Meg also nodded. "Are you," she coughed, "mad at me?"

"*Mad* at you? Of course not, Meg—why would I be?"

"Because"—Meg couldn't look at her— "I was such a jerk that day. About the sweat pants, I mean."

Her mother looked confused, then smiled. "Don't tell me you're worried about *that.*"

"Well, yeah. I mean—yeah."

Her mother laughed. "Really not to worry, Meg. I'd completely forgotten."

"I didn't mean to be such a jerk to you, I—"

"Yeah, you did," her mother said. "You just didn't mean for anything *bad* to happen."

"Yeah, but—" Meg swallowed, her throat hurting. "I was in physics and I hadn't studied for the test and—I was

196

wishing for a fire drill, or something to get me out of there. *Anything.*"

Her mother smiled, putting her hand on Meg's shoulder. "It doesn't mean you wanted anything to happen to *me*."

"Well, yeah, but—"

"Just forget it," her mother said. "Worrying about something like that is pointless."

"But—really?"

Her mother nodded.

"Are you—scared?"

Her mother studied her sling. "In some ways," she said. "It's not going to be debilitating though."

Meg looked at her thoughtfully. "Can I ask you something?"

"You *may*," her mother said.

"Something, um, sort of unfriendly?"

Her mother nodded uneasily.

"How come you were such a jerk when you left the hospital? You were like, *waiting* for someone to shoot you."

A muscle in her mother's cheek twitched. "I gather you saw a film clip."

Meg nodded.

"Well." She sat on Meg's bed, hunching again.

"What if something had happened?"

"I suppose the hospital would have checked me right back in."

Meg shook her head. "It's not funny."

"No. It isn't."

"Yeah, well, something could have happened. I mean, weren't you thinking about *us?*"

"No," her mother said and Meg blinked. "I was thinking about how scared I was and how I wasn't going to let anyone in the whole goddamn country know that."

Her mother never swore.

"Yeah, but—" Meg moved her hair back over her shoulders. "Something could have happened."

Her mother shrugged, wincing almost simultaneously. "Then, I suppose it would have."

"Yeah, but—" Meg shook her head impatiently. "You don't have to go *looking* for it."

"Yes," her mother said. "Sometimes I do."

It was quiet as Meg thought about that. "Terrific," she said. "That's—that's just terrific."

"It's part of my job, Meg."

"Great," Meg said. "And we all just sit around, waiting for the next bad thing to happen."

"If that's the way you want to live."

Meg stared at her, irritated. "I don't get it. Don't you care at all?"

"For the rest of my life," her mother's voice was low, "every time I change my clothes, I'm going to have to think about it. Every time—" She shook her head. "Let's put it this way. Off-the-shoulder dresses are a thing of my past."

Meg looked at her, for the first time thinking about physical scars. The ones that *did* show.

"When you're trying to save the President's life," her mother said, "the cosmetic aspects of it all are certainly not on your list of priorities."

The mood in the room was so unhappy that Meg decided to risk a joke. "Well," she sat taller, even being a little sultry, "it looks like I'm in line for a lot of nice clothes."

"Over my dead body," her mother said, and Meg flinched. It was briefly silent; then, unexpectedly, her mother grinned. "A rather unfortunate witticism," she said.

"Yeah," Meg said.

"And yet," her mother's voice was solemn, her eyes amused, "appropriate in its way."

"That's sick," Meg said. "That's just plain sick."

"Yes," her mother agreed. "Rather." She looked at Meg, her eyes bright with amusement, and Meg had to laugh, her mother relaxing and joining in. It was loud laughing, and Meg felt out of practice.

"The—" She tried to stop. "The blue dress. You know, the one you wore for the astronaut thing. Can I—" She couldn't stop—"Can I have that?"

Her mother stopped laughing. "My blue dress? I love that dress."

"Well, yeah," Meg said. "But if you're not going to be using it . . ."

"No," her mother said. "I'm not giving you that dress." Her grin was self-amused. "It's *mine.*"

"The dog said, from her manger."

Her mother laughed. "Damn straight."

"Oh," Meg nodded. "You seem to have acquired quite the gutter mouth."

"Yes," her mother said, using *her* formal voice. "That appears to be the case."

They looked at each other, grinning.

"No *way* do you get that dress," her mother said.

"Thank you," Meg said. "I applaud your generosity."

Her mother laughed, coming over to hug her with one arm. "I suppose I'm taking you from your work," she said, not straightening up right away.

"Yes," Meg said. "Rather."

CHAPTER TWENTY-TWO

Thanksgiving was wonderful. Peaceful. Quiet. Relaxed. Meg did a lot of hiking around with Kirby, and once he even fetched a stick. Agents and staff people lurked all over the place, but her parents had prepared a list of supplies, and the kitchen in their cabin had been stocked with Thanksgiving food since her parents had arranged to do the cooking themselves. As usual, her father did most of the work, her mother being a backseat driver about it, and Meg heard a lot of laughing from the kitchen. Steven shot baskets and played one-on-one with agents. Neal played Atari. Her parents had broken down and given it to him for his birthday, with the stipulation that he only use it at Camp David so that his mind, and his eyesight, wouldn't completely degenerate. Considering the hours he spent playing, they probably had a point.

They left Washington on Wednesday, flying up in the presidential helicopter, returning to the White House on Sunday. Josh came over that night and they went down to the projection room to watch *War Games* with her brothers. It was one of her brothers' favorite movies, but her mother had never been able to sit all the way through it. Steven got a charge out of walking around the house and remarking at odd moments, "Let's play Global Thermonuclear War," speaking slowly and solemnly. Because of the Atari set at Camp David, he had probably said it about thirty times over the weekend. Her parents thought that was in bad taste.

It was kind of fun to be able to sit in a movie theater in the *house,* especially because the chairs in the front row were so comfortable and Felix, or whoever was on duty, would deliver popcorn; but the projection room was for lounging, rather than being romantic. When Josh was around, Meg generally felt like being romantic. The front row easy chairs were so far apart that they could really only hold hands, which they would never do in front of Steven and Neal. Sometimes, when they were watching movies alone, they would sit in the same easy chair, Meg mostly on Josh's lap, but that would end up being too distracting for serious movie-watching.

After the movie, which Steven and Neal decided to watch again, Meg and Josh wandered around, ending up in the solarium, Felix having given them a plate of brownies, as well as Tab and Coke. They put *The Sound of Music*—which was Meg's favorite movie in life—in the VCR and sat on the couch to watch. Once the movie started, Meg felt unexpectedly restless.

"What's with you?" Josh asked.

"I don't know."

"I thought this was your favorite movie in life."

"It is. I just—I don't know."

He put his arm around her and she moved closer, running her hand along the side of his jaw which felt smooth, but solid. That was good—men were supposed to have nice solid jaws. Actually, it was probably a good idea for everyone to have a nice solid jaw, but you were supposed to notice it in men.

"When was the last time you shaved?" she asked.

"I don't know. Two weeks ago."

"That must be pretty potent after-shave then."

He grinned, but didn't elaborate.

"It'll probably take you about six years to go through a bottle."

"Probably," he agreed.

"You have hair on your chest though. That means there's still hope."

"Probably," he agreed.

"You want me to shut up and watch the movie?"

"Yeah."

"Okay." She was quiet for a scene or two, watching the nuns, then turned her head to kiss his neck, working her way up to his mouth. His attention abruptly left the movie, and his other arm came around her.

"I've seen this movie about six hundred times," he said.

"Yeah, me too."

They kept kissing.

"Oh, wait," Meg tried to sit up. "I want to watch this part." She grinned at his expression. "Of course, it's not *imperative.*"

"Jerk," he said and started tickling her, which made both of them laugh. Actually, except with the opposite sex, Meg had never been particularly ticklish. Oh, and doctors. Doctors almost always set her off. Her pediatrician had said that he loved to treat her because she made him feel like such an amusing person.

"Cut it out," she said, laughing weakly.

He stopped right away, which she thought was nice. Some people would tickle you all day.

"If you'd rather watch the movie . . ." he said, kissing her.

"No, thanks. Unless you'd rather."

"No, thanks."

She ran her hands through his hair, feeling the shape of his skull. What a nice skull. She pulled away.

"Hey, wouldn't this be a good time to hear some jokes?" she asked. "I know some really good jokes."

"Can I hear them after?"

"After what?"

He started tickling her again and she agreed to stop being a pain. But suddenly, all of this seemed terribly funny, and after another minute or so, she pulled away.

"Do you mind if I wear your glasses for a while?" she asked.

He lifted himself onto one elbow to look at her. "Are you getting in a weird mood?"

She nodded.

"Your weird moods drive me crazy."

"I don't have them often."

"Often enough."

"Boy, what a grump." She hugged him, pulling him back down.

"I'm not a grump."

"Yeah, you are. Grump, grump, grump, grump—" She decided to stop talking. Funny to think she had gone through a period when the concept of French kissing was too gross to be believed. Ah, the wisdom of eleven-year-olds. Or like that song Lauren Bacall sang in *To Have and Have Not:* "How Little We Know . . ." She loved *To Have and Have Not.* In fact, maybe she would be Lauren Bacall for a while. "Steve?" she asked, her voice low and sexy.

Josh frowned at her. "Steve?"

"Aw, come on, Steve." She pushed his cheek playfully. "Don't be mad, Steve."

"I'm not—"

She pushed his other cheek. "You're mad. Admit it, Steve." She folded her hands behind his head. "Kiss me, Steve."

He grinned. "Your voice is too high."

"I think not, Steve," she said, trying for a deep throaty rasp.

"Better," he nodded and she tried to kiss him the way Lauren Bacall would. Only now that she thought about it, Lauren Bacall—and anyone else—would probably be wise to stay away from Josh. Not that she was possessive or anything.

"Got a match, Slim?" Josh asked, playing Humphrey Bogart now.

Us. Only that was too stupid to actually say. It was the kind of thing you could think to your heart's content, but would almost always be too cool to say. Sort of like "I love you."

"Was you ever bit by a dead bee?" Josh asked, still playing *To Have and Have Not.*

Meg didn't answer, touching his face, moving her hands back through his hair. People talked about "I love you" being really trite. Then, how come saying it was such a big deal? Better question: how come *she* was such a coward about saying it?

"Hey." Josh tapped her cheek. "Wake up. You missed your cue."

"Yeah." She shook her head. "Sorry."

"What are you thinking about?"

"I don't know. Nothing, I guess."

He shifted onto his side and she adjusted her position accordingly, her arm trapped under his weight.

"You think a lot," he said.

"Not really. It just takes me longer."

He laughed, brushing her hair away from her face. Long hair had a tendency to get in the way of amorous encounters. "You're cute," he said.

"Thank you. So are you."

"Thank you." He lifted himself slightly. "Your arm must be falling asleep."

"Yeah, kind of." She extricated it, then looked at his eyes, every dot of the light brown pigment familiar. "I love you."

He blinked. "Because I saved your arm?" he asked, sounding as if he were only half-kidding.

"No. I mean, not *just* that," she corrected herself. "I mean—well, for lots of reasons. I mean—I don't know. I just love you." She closed her eyes. "I have to rest now."

He laughed and she smelled after-shave as he bent his head to kiss her cheek. "I love you too," he said. "Very much."

CHAPTER TWENTY-THREE

The last hurdle, Meg figured, was the *Seventeen* interview. She had had a pretty tough time with the first one. Preston set the new one up for the Thursday she didn't have play rehearsal—she was running lights—so she could come home right after school and get ready. Get psyched, as Nathan would say.

She woke up in a wonderful mood that morning, so cheerful that she wore the Williams sweatshirt she had gotten when she and her father visited colleges.

"Oh," her mother said when she walked into the dining room for breakfast.

"Nice shirt, huh?" Meg sat down, taking the Cheerios box away from Neal, pouring herself some, and reading the back.

"Dad!" Neal protested.

"Meg, give him the box," her father said patiently.

Meg sighed the deepest sigh she could manage and handed it to him.

"Yeah, thanks," Neal grumbled.

"You're welcome," Meg said graciously. *"De rien."*

"French," Steven snorted. "How queer."

"Tu es un chien laid," Meg said.

Her parents looked at her.

"What?" Steven asked. "What did she call me?"

"A handsome and talented basketball player," their mother said. What a diplomat. Her sling had been off for almost a week now and she could use her left arm, albeit gingerly.

Meg helped herself to some toast. *"Il est un grostesque—"*

"Is she calling me gross?" Steven demanded, looking from one parent to the other.

"Mais oui." Meg nodded. *"Tu es un—"*

"All right," her father said, laughing. "Enough already. Eat your breakfasts."

"Forse, la figlia non sia bellissima," her mother remarked.

They all looked at her.

"A meundo, es vergonzoso estar visto con ella," she said.

"My God, she's speaking in tongues!" Meg said. "Call a priest!"

"Je suis la Présidente," her mother said blandly and winked at Meg's father. *"Je peux faire n'importe quoi."*

"Mommy, what are you saying?" Neal asked, Cheerios box forgotten.

"That you are one of my two favorite sons."

"But *I'm* the very favorite child," Meg said.

"No way," Steven said. "You're too ugly."

"You're about ten times uglier."

"Yeah, you wish, chick. Your whole room's full of broken mirrors."

"Because you sneak in there when I'm not around."

"No way," Steven said. "You're *so* ugly—" He paused for effect.

"How ugly is she?" Neal asked, already laughing.

"So ugly that like, the Queen was like, throwing up the whole time she was here."

Their father put down his fork. "Steven, the Queen hasn't been here."

"That's 'cause she's scared she might throw up," Steven said without hesitating, and even Meg had to laugh.

"It's true," their mother said. "I've invited her several times."

Meg stopped eating her cereal. "How come everyone's picking on me all of a sudden?"

"Because you're so ugly," Steven said.

Meg considered that, then took a bite of toast and jam, following it with a bite of cereal, then chewing to make a very unpleasant mess and opening her mouth to show it to Steven.

"Stop right there," her father said, but he didn't sound very irritated. "You know I don't like that game."

Meg closed her mouth and nodded sadly. From across the table, Steven showed her an equally disgusting mouthful and she laughed so hard that she had to gulp half her orange juice to stop choking.

"Now just stop it," her father said. "I really don't like that."

"Stop choking?" Meg asked, laughing. "I don't like it much either."

He frowned at her, but his eyes were amused. "Try to behave like a mature young woman," he suggested and Steven laughed raucously.

"Notice he didn't call *you* mature," Meg said.

"That's 'cause he didn't feel like he had to," Steven said, shrugging. "He knows I'm a man."

"*Munchkin* man," Meg said.

"Isn't it about time for all of you to go to school?" their mother asked.

"Not me!" Neal said.

"No, not you," their mother agreed. "It seems to me that it's time for your brother and sister to leave though."

"Boy," Meg said. "Can tell when *we're* not wanted."

"Yeah," Steven said. "*Neal's* the favorite."

"I am not!" Neal said.

"Boy," Meg pushed her cereal away. "Let's go find an audience who will appreciate us, Steven."

"Try the zoo," her father suggested.

"Boy, they don't even love us," Steven said. He clapped Neal on the shoulder. "Take notes on what they say about us, son. We'll quiz you later."

"You know, I bet you would," their mother said thoughtfully.

Meg and Steven laughed evil laughs.

At school, her good mood got even better and she had so much trouble sitting still in her classes that she got yelled at three times. This amused her even more. The choir was selling Christmas and Hanukkah cards now, which weren't as much fun to throw, but they made do with crumpled pieces of paper. None of their teachers enjoyed it.

At lunch, they were still rowdier, throwing around French fries and Zachary's olives. The teacher on duty yelled at them and they spent the rest of the lunch being as dignified as possible and laughing a lot. Mr. Murphy got so mad during Current Issues that he almost kept them after school, but luckily, he didn't. Having to call Preston and tell him that she would be late to the interview because she had detention would be kind of embarrassing.

After her agents dropped her off on the ground floor, Meg making jokes with them, she went to change into conservative clothing, and was ready twenty minutes early. She paced up and down the hall, as pleasantly jittery as she was before tennis matches on days when she knew she was going to play well. The chief usher intercepted her in the East Sitting Hall.

"Mr. Fielding is on his way upstairs," he said.

"Oh, thank you." She walked—ran—swiftly down to the West Sitting Hall to jitter around and wait for them. She looked out the window, and to be whimsical, waved at the Oval Office. Too bad Vanessa wasn't around. But Humphrey was sitting on the coffee table and she lifted his front paws to dance with him briefly.

"Good afternoon, Miss Powers," Preston said.

She released Humphrey, who began washing to recover dignity. She just blushed. "Um, good afternoon."

"Good afternoon," Ms. Wright said, smiling.

They all sat down and Meg resisted an urge to swing her feet onto the coffee table and be cocky as hell. George came, and Meg decided to have coffee along with the others. How adult. She would endeavor to be sly about the many sugars she put in.

"I'm very sorry about what happened," Ms. Wright said.

Meg nodded. "Thank you. Things are much better now."

"That's good to hear." Ms. Wright uncapped her felt-tip pen. "I'm also sorry about the way the interview went last time."

"I think it was my fault," Meg said. "I'm not very good at this."

"I'd say that you're extremely good at it." Ms. Wright scanned her note pad, then looked up with a smile. "I'll start you off easily, Meg. Tell me how you're feeling these days."

"Pretty good," Meg said. Then, she grinned. "Maybe even great."

ELLEN EMERSON WHITE grew up in Naragansett, Rhode Island. She graduated from Tufts University in 1983 and now lives on Manhattan's Upper West Side with her dog, Zachary, and her cat, Nicholas.